RIVALRIES, CONFLICTS . . .
DISASTER!

SARAH wasn't about to let Phil think she couldn't keep up with a man. But she never expected their *lives* to be in her hands . . .

PHIL wanted to prove to Sarah that he was a real man. But he was even more interested in proving it to the other men . . .

MIKE was self-assured, good-looking, and very appealing to Sarah. Until his macho one-upmanship drove them all to disaster . . .

DIANNE adored Mike, even though he played around every chance he got. When she lost him, her world fell apart . . .

JIM was easy going and let his wife get the better of him once too often. This time she pushed him too far . . .

RACHEL acted tough to hide the broken feelings inside of her. But how tough would she be in the wilderness without Jim?

INTO THE BACK COUNTRY

Maurice L'Heureux

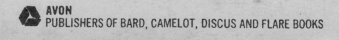
AVON
PUBLISHERS OF BARD, CAMELOT, DISCUS AND FLARE BOOKS

INTO THE BACK COUNTRY is an original publication of Avon Books. This work has never before appeared in book form.

AVON BOOKS
A division of
The Hearst Corporation
959 Eighth Avenue
New York, New York 10019

Copyright © 1983 by Maurice L'Heureux
Published by arrangement with the author
Library of Congress Catalog Card Number: 82-90479
ISBN: 0-380-81588-5

First Avon Printing, January, 1983

AVON TRADEMARK REG. U. S. PAT. OFF. AND IN OTHER COUNTRIES, MARCA REGISTRADA, HECHO EN U. S. A.

Printed in the U. S. A.

WFH 10 9 8 7 6 5 4 3 2 1

INTO THE
BACK
COUNTRY

Day One

Sarah's nightshirt was twisted from a restless sleep.

Drawing a deep breath, she struggled to the edge of the bed and sat up.

She instinctively reached for her cigarettes, and, after staring at the wall a minute or two, sucking smoke, waiting for her brain to come on line, she stepped into her new hiking boots.

Only forty minutes left, she thought. Why are you always rushing someplace you don't want to go?

Feeling stale and prematurely old, Sarah threw on her robe and walked stiff-legged to the bathroom. She turned on the shower; then, as she undressed, she noticed the spotting in her underwear.

Terrific, she thought. That's just what you need.

When Sarah stepped into the shower, the first blast of steamy water made her purr with contentment. She knew that it would be her last shower for a week, so she had to drag herself away.

She went to the full-length mirror on the back of the door and dried off.

Sarah Keller was a small woman, a little over five feet tall, with sandy-colored hair that frizzled up like steel wool whenever it rained. Her eyes were hazy blue and opened wide as if she were constantly surprised.

So the breasts could be larger, she thought. And the knees aren't too great. So what? It's inner beauty that counts in this world.

The hell it is.

Sarah had no pretensions about her looks. She knew that in the meat market of dating, she was round steak among the sirloin. Still, it was better than being hamburger.

Her husband, Gary, used to get excited about her—at least during the first years of their marriage. Near the end,

7

he would look at her like an old pair of jeans that would soon have to be thrown away.

Too bad Gary turned out to be such a shit.

When Sarah was dried off, she hot-combed her hair, then returned to the bedroom to get dressed.

As she lit her second cigarette of the day, she examined the clothes that Phil and Mike had selected for her. Mike Stove said that wool was the best, so, of course, wool it was —wool shirt, wool slacks, wool socks. The cold-weather hiking gear cost her a bundle and made Sarah wish she had gone to Florida instead.

Why did she let Phil talk her into doing things she didn't want to do?

The clothes were a waste of money, but the boots looked okay, and she thought she could wear them when she got back to New York. With a pair of designer jeans they weren't half bad.

For the past two weeks she had worn the boots everywhere except bed in order to break them in. She would take them to the office in a paper bag, and, at lunch, put them on in the restroom and go for long walks in the city.

By the time Sarah was into her fishnet underwear, wool pants, wool shirt, wool socks, and wool sweater, she was already exhausted and sweaty.

Only twenty minutes! she thought.

The kitchen of her apartment was cluttered with the leftovers and dirty dishes from the birthday dinner Phil had made.

It was a good dinner; in fact, the whole evening had gone well, she thought, as she rifled through the cabinets for her powdered breakfast drink.

Why hadn't Phil told her before that he knew how to cook?

The best part of the evening was that Phil had talked a lot about himself—something he rarely did—and Sarah had felt close to him.

Perhaps she was making too many unfair comparisons.

Clomping through the kitchen in her hiking boots, Sarah went to the refrigerator and looked inside.

No milk.

What would instant breakfast powder taste like on toast? It was foolish to leave without eating anything.

In desperation, Sarah nibbled on a cold chicken leg, but she soon lost her appetite.

There was one more ritual to perform before Sarah could leave—she had to feed the cat. Sarah had arranged to have the old woman across the hall take care of Christabel while she was gone.

Sarah and Christabel stuck to their routine faithfully. After Sarah dressed for work, she would go to the wicker basket next to the sofa and stroke Christabel's belly. On cue, the cat would stretch, then slowly get up and follow Sarah to the feeding bowl.

But this morning the routine was shattered—Christabel was gone.

In mild shock, Sarah raced around the apartment searching for her cat. Christabel was more than a pet. She was an anniversary present from Gary the year they moved to New York so that Gary could attend medical school.

First came the cat. Then came the divorce. Christabel was the only thing Sarah had left from her life with Gary.

Sarah looked everywhere—the bathtub, the kitchen cabinets, under the sofa, but still no cat.

The doorbell rang, and she went to answer it.

Phil was standing there dressed in brand-new slacks, flannel shirt, and green hunter's vest. His face was soft and young looking for a man of forty, but the beginnings of a spare tire crept over his belt.

"Christabel's gone," Sarah said.

"Gone where?"

"I don't know. She's just gone."

"For Christ's sake," Phil said, "everyone's waiting for us."

"Then help me look for the cat."

Cursing under his breath, Phil got down on his hands and knees and crawled around the floor, searching under the furniture.

"You ought to have that damn thing put to sleep," he said after a while.

Sarah grew more desperate as the minutes went by and still there was no sign of Christabel. It was so nice to come home tired from work, curl up next to the cat, stroke her soft fur, and listen to the soothing hum of Christabel's motor.

It was more effective than the meditation class Sarah had attended after the divorce.

"It's no use," Phil said angrily as he got up from the floor, sweat dripping from his nose.

"I can't leave until I know she's all right," Sarah said.

"Then you stay here and look for the cat, and I'll go on the trip."

"Do you always have to be such a jerk?"

"You're the one who's making everyone late."

"I'm going to look in the basement," Sarah said. "Christabel tried to get down there yesterday."

Before Phil could stop her, Sarah had bolted out the door and was heading fast down the stairwell.

"Damn that cat anyway!" Phil shouted. Then he took off after Sarah.

When they entered the apartment basement, it was difficult to see. The windows were smoky and blocked by newspapers in the alley.

"I've asked the manager a hundred times to fix the lights down here," Sarah said. "You can't do the wash without a baseball bat in your hand."

"Just hurry up."

Sarah led the way as they stumbled past dryers and washing machines. Phil crashed into a support post and cursed aloud as he rubbed his forehead.

Sarah continued to look for her cat, but it appeared useless.

She was just about to give up the search when she heard a sharp cry from the utility closet on the other side of the room.

"Is that Christabel?" Sarah asked. "It doesn't sound like her."

They went to the closet, and Phil lit a match so they could see better. Then he threw open the closet door, and they discovered Christabel with the hind end of a rat dangling from her mouth.

Sarah was so revolted by the grotesque scene that she gagged when she spoke.

"Get her out of there, Phil."

He reached inside for the cat, but Christabel raked his hand with her paws and drew blood.

"I ought to kill her!" he yelled, sucking his wound.

He tried to grab the cat once again, and this time Christabel jumped out from the closet and ran out of sight into the far end of the basement.

10

"We have to leave her," Phil said. "We don't have any more time to fool around."

But Sarah didn't want Christabel back now. She was disgusted with the cat.

"I don't care what happens to her," she said.

"Good. Let's get out of here."

Phil and Sarah walked back through the maze of washing machines, up the stairs, and into the apartment. Before leaving, Sarah had a change of heart and scribbled a note to the neighbor asking her to keep an eye out for the cat.

Then Phil picked up Sarah's backpack, and they went outside to join the others.

"What the hell took you so long?" Mike asked as he and Dianne loosened the tarp on the roof of the van.

"Sarah's cat ran away," Phil said. "We couldn't catch her."

"You couldn't catch a little cat?"

"You know how they get sometimes."

"Still," Mike said with a teasing grin, "it was only a cat."

Phil threw the backpack hard into Mike's arms.

Sarah had met Mike and his wife before, but she was impressed again by what a gorgeous pair they made. Mike was tall and big-shouldered, with blue eyes, close-cropped black hair, and the kind of devilishly cute smile that Sarah was always a sucker for. Mike was wearing the same outfit as Phil, but Mike's clothes looked worn and seemed more natural on him.

Dianne was a slender, no-makeup kind of woman with a glowing pink complexion that made her look almost feverish. She had long blonde hair with the type of controlled curl that Sarah had always wanted.

"We're running late," Mike said. "Let's go."

Mike and Dianne sat in the front of the van while Sarah and Phil joined the Wheatleys in the back.

"You remember Rachel, don't you?" Phil asked Sarah. "You met her at the office party last Christmas."

"Of course she remembers me," Rachel said. "Sarah and I had a nice little talk while you and Jim swam in the punch bowl."

"I swam thirty laps," Jim said. "My breast stroke's improving."

"I'll believe that when I feel it," Rachel said.

Rachel had a strong, unrefined type of beauty. Her black

11

hair was pulled back tightly, and her plucked eyebrows gave her a stern appearance.

Her husband, Jim, was tall and lanky with an equally lanky personality. Sarah found him easy to talk to, friendly, and unpretentious.

"Would you like a Bloody Mary?" Jim asked after Mike had pulled out onto the highway.

"Not me," Phil said. "I drank too much wine last night."

"What was the occasion?"

"It was Sarah's birthday," Phil said. "She's thirty-two."

"He didn't ask how old I was," Sarah said.

"You're still a kid," Jim said. "Cheer up and have a drink with me to celebrate."

It was shortly after six A.M., and Sarah hadn't had anything to eat.

"No thanks," she said. "I normally wait until it's light enough to see."

"Then it's up to me," Jim said, pouring a hefty amount of vodka into a paper cup with just enough tomato juice to give it some color.

He drank the Bloody Mary quickly.

"Jim will celebrate anything," Rachel said. "One day he celebrated Saint Patrick's Day in the middle of July."

"It was a memorable day," Jim said.

"The only thing I remember is picking you up from the tank after you got caught pissing on the Cathedral steps."

"It was something I always wanted to do. Since when did you start holding back on compulsions?"

Rachel didn't answer.

Sarah felt sorry for Jim in spite of his outward appearance of good humor. Ever since the divorce, she took more notice of people with wounds you couldn't see.

Mike Stove announced to the group that they would arrive at their destination around eight o'clock. They would sleep in a wilderness lodge run by a friend he had gone hunting with the year before.

The more Mike and Dianne talked about backpacking and the wilderness, the more excited Sarah became. Their love for the back country was infectious. Sarah could feel the reverence in their voices as they described their trips to the Grand Tetons, the Cascades, and the Appalachian Trail. It was as if the Stoves shared a vital secret between them, and now they were going to share that secret with their friends.

12

If backpacking would make Sarah anything like Dianne Stove, she was anxious to give it a try. At this stage, Sarah was ready to try anything.

Mike Stove filled the tedious hours of the trip with his vast knowledge of backpacking and nature. He talked about everything from calculating the temperature from the number of cricket chirps to predicting the weather from the shape and density of clouds.

"It takes a while to get to know the back country," Mike said, "but once you do, you can survive anything."

Sarah liked the way the Stoves often touched each other and seemed interested in what the other person was saying. There was a strong sensuality about the two of them, even after ten years of marriage and two children.

How could they be so excited about each other after sleeping together a few thousand times?

The more Sarah watched the Stoves, the more she became jealous of their marriage.

The Wheatleys' relationship seemed as rocky as the Stoves' was strong. Though Jim and Rachel had been together for some time, there wasn't any warmth between them. When they talked to each other, it was as if they were bored, and Rachel's humor always made Jim look like a clown.

But Jim never appeared to mind.

"I heard you were divorced not too long ago," Rachel said to Sarah.

"A year."

"I've been divorced twice. It gets easier each time."

"I'll take your word for it."

"I don't want to be nosy," Rachel said, "but what happened?"

"It hurts to talk about it."

"Sometimes it can be fun."

"Maybe later it will be."

Twice more during the drive, Rachel tried to get Sarah to talk about her divorce, but Sarah changed the subject both times.

It had been easier to talk about Gary when Sarah was angry, but she wasn't angry anymore. Depressed, yes. Confused, yes. Angry, no.

Phil spent a lot of time talking to Mike Stove about hiking and hunting. Though Mike was five years younger, Phil looked up to him like an older brother. Also like brothers, there was an adolescent competition between them that Sarah found embarrassing.

"Did you know that Sarah was born with a hole in her heart?" Phil asked Mike.

Sarah wanted to kill him on the spot. She had shared her childhood problem with Phil only after he had sworn to keep his mouth shut about it.

"Why did you tell him that?" Sarah said angrily.

"I thought it was interesting."

Mike looked over his shoulder at Sarah with an expression of deep concern. "I hope there's nothing wrong with you now."

"Of course there isn't."

She punched Phil in the arm. "See what you've done? They think I'm on my last leg."

"They do not."

Sarah caught Mike's attention in the rear-view mirror.

"I was a little girl," she explained. "The hole was fixed, and there hasn't been any problem since."

"I was going to add that," Phil interrupted.

He tried to put his arm around Sarah, but she brushed him off.

"This hike will be good for us," Mike said, changing the subject. "It will give us a chance to get in tune with our bodies."

"That's great," Rachel said. "Jim's body could use a tune-up. In fact, a new engine wouldn't hurt."

"I'm serious. We forget about our bodies at work. They get flabby. Hiking changes that."

"I can't believe it makes that much of a difference," Rachel said.

"It even improves your sex life. You'll notice it when you get back to New York."

"Now you're talking Rachel's language," Jim said.

"A man who can't handle himself in the wilderness is only half a man," Mike said.

"Jim already handles himself too much," Rachel said. "That's part of our problem."

"Isn't hiking important for women, too?" Sarah asked. "I don't know why you restrict it to men."

"Hiking's good for you, too," Mike said, "but it's more vital for a man."

14

"Of course it is," Phil said. "Man's the hunter. He's the provider."

"Do you really believe that?" Sarah asked.

"We can't overlook what's right in front of us. Men have superior strength, better upper body development, a different center of gravity."

"I think that your center of gravity is hanging over your belt a little too far," Sarah said.

Everyone laughed, except Phil.

"We're only talking about different roles," Dianne continued to argue. "One isn't superior to the other."

"I still don't buy it," Sarah said. "Women have proven they're just as competent as men in every field."

"That's true in the city," Mike said, "because it's an artificial environment. But you get out in the wilderness and it's a different story."

"He's right," Phil said.

Sarah took note of Phil's smug expression. Perhaps she wasn't being too cautious about him after all.

The drive was long and boring, and Sarah kept waiting for the scenery to get interesting. There was nothing but mile after mile of farmland, and even after they entered Canada the landscape continued to be flat and unimpressive.

Sarah hoped that after all the trouble she had gone through, and all the money she had spent on hiking clothes, she wasn't going to be disappointed when they arrived. Where were the "natural highs" that the Stoves spoke about? The only thing changing so far was the temperature.

It wasn't until evening, well past Montreal, that the land changed dramatically. The tract houses, shopping centers, and traffic faded away, and they entered a region of endless rolling hills that were covered with what Sarah thought were Christmas trees. Soon, promising signs like MOOSEHEAD LAKE and NIGHTHAWK RESERVE began to appear along the roadway.

Some of the group wanted to stop for dinner, but Mike refused. "We only stop if one of you has to use the can," he said.

"You're a cruel man," Jim Wheatley said.

"You have to get used to roughing it sooner or later."

When darkness came to the forest, Sarah realized how

15

truly isolated they were. They hadn't passed a car in a long time, and the darkness was more complete than Sarah had ever seen it, especially in the city.

Jim and Rachel were sprawled out on separate seats in the van, covered up by their down parkas. Dianne was asleep on Mike's shoulder. Phil was snoring peacefully with his head nestled on Sarah's lap.

In the green glow of the dashboard, Sarah could see Mike's determined expression. He stared at the road as if he were attacking it.

It reminded Sarah of the way her father used to drive all night to get a head start on vacation. Sarah always felt warm and safe as she watched her father keep his lonely vigil at the wheel. She felt that way now.

Phil woke up, and Sarah told him to speak softly. He sat and spread a blanket over their legs.

"Look at all the stars," Phil said, looking out the window of the van. "It reminds me of our weekend at Cape Cod."

"You still remember that?"

"Of course I do. We set a record—we didn't fight for two days."

"We're not that bad."

Sarah pointed out the window and said, "That's the Big Dipper."

"And that must be Venus. The bright star over there."

Phil cleaned the fog off the window with his sleeve, so they could see better. As he did, he gave Sarah a kiss.

Sarah enjoyed the warm, close feeling of being under the covers together.

She rubbed the stubble on Phil's face.

"Did you shave this morning?" she asked him.

"I'm starting to grow a beard."

"Why?"

"Beards and camping go together."

He touched Sarah's hair and twisted some of it around his finger.

"I'm going to get in shape," Phil said. "I want my weight down to where it was a few years ago."

"I wouldn't mind that," Sarah said.

"It's time to deflate this spare tire."

Sarah poked her finger into his side.

"I don't know," she said. "A little pudginess makes you cute."

16

"I want to be in shape, not cute."

Phil put his arm around her.

"Canada would make a nice place to honeymoon," he said.

"Don't start that again."

"You always talk about marriage like it's an ordeal."

"Mine was."

Sarah wondered how many times they had been through this stupid, futile discussion. The one thing she knew for certain in her life was that marriage was out of the question—at least for now.

"There's no rush," Sarah said.

"Not for you, but I'm forty."

"So what?"

"Turning forty makes you think. I remember when my father was fifty, I thought he was a fossil."

"You've got plenty of years left."

"Most of my friends are married and have kids. There was a time when I didn't want that, but now I do."

"What can I say? It's not for me. Not now."

"Tell me honestly. Does my age have anything to do with why you won't marry me?"

"I won't even answer a dumb question like that."

Sarah looked outside at the dark outline of the tree tops. The moon was barely visible behind a passing cloud. There was a pocket of fog trapped between two hills.

"It's good that we'll be spending so much time together," Sarah said to Phil. "You might change your mind about me."

"That's not going to happen."

Sarah took her cigarettes out of her shirt pocket and lit up.

"I wish you wouldn't smoke so much," Phil said.

"Don't lecture me."

"I'm worried about you. I want you to stay alive."

"You act like I'm a real prize."

"You are a prize."

"And you're a cornball."

Phil smiled and gave her another kiss. Then he lay back down on the seat and rested his head in Sarah's lap. She covered him up with a blanket.

As she looked down at Phil, Sarah knew she wanted to remarry someday. She was lonely by herself, and just living with a man seemed too provisional and cowardly. But the idea of going through another bad marriage was terrifying enough to make her prefer the loneliness.

Sometimes she was embarrassed by how calculating she had become in her relationships—measuring the risk of investments, studying the market, looking for the highest yields. But you got that way after a divorce. You didn't want to get hurt again.

In a way, Sarah felt sorry for Phil. If he had been the first one to propose, she probably would have married him. But she was smarter now, and Phil would have to suffer for it, even though she didn't want him to.

Somewhere along the line, and not too far off, she was going to have to make a final decision about him.

Mike Stove pulled into the parking lot of Pohick Lodge shortly after eight, exactly on schedule.

"Wake up!" he shouted to his sleeping crew.

Everyone yawned and stretched.

"Let's stay here all week," Jim said. "We won't wear out our shoes."

"It must be freezing," Rachel said. "Look at the frost on the windows."

Mike and Phil left the van to go register in the lodge while the others unloaded the gear from the top rack.

It had been a long day's ride, and when Sarah stepped outside the ground still seemed to be moving.

The hikers stamped their feet on the ground and rubbed their hands for warmth.

The lodge was the only source of light as far as the eye could see. It looked pitiably small surrounded by the immense dark forest.

"I can't believe that we're going to sleep out there," Sarah said as she stared into the trees.

"That must be the restaurant," Jim said, pointing to a neon sign at one end of the lodge. "Let's hurry up and get inside."

Dianne and Rachel climbed up onto the roof of the van and handed down the packs to Jim and Sarah.

Suddenly a pickup truck roared into the gravel lot and skidded to a stop inches away.

The doors flew open, and two men in baggy pants and orange hunters' caps stumbled out. One of them fell at Sarah's feet.

"Hello, ma'am," he said with a drunken smile.

He dragged himself from the ground and bowed to Sarah in mock formality, taking off his cap. His breath was sour, his eyes watery. He turned to his friend now and shouted, "Hey, Bill. Let's take these girls inside to dance."

"You bet, Lenny."

Bill reached up and tried to pull Dianne from the roof of the van, but she crawled back out of reach.

"Get lost," Rachel said.

At that moment, the one called Lenny grabbed Sarah's wrist and pulled her to the rear of the truck. He threw down the battered tailgate and revealed a dead deer.

"You ever seen a fresh-killed doe?" he asked Sarah.

The animal's belly was slit open top to bottom with nothing but a dark cavity inside. Sarah was shocked by the sight and tried to pull herself free, but Lenny pressed her hand against the blood-soaked fur.

"Stroke it," Lenny said. "It's as smooth as pussy."

Rachel jumped down from the roof of the van and tried to go to Sarah's aide, but the man called Bill grabbed her from behind and held her as she kicked and squirmed.

Sarah noticed Dianne jump off the van during the confusion and run toward the lodge.

"These girls are wildcats!" Bill said.

"Let go of me," Sarah said.

"You're not very friendly," Lenny said.

Sarah was scared, but she didn't want Lenny to see it.

"You might think this is fun, but I don't," she said.

Lenny broke out laughing, and Sarah—before she knew what she was doing—spat in his face.

"Why, you little bitch," Lenny said as he wiped the spit out of his eyes. "You're gonna get yours now!"

Suddenly Bill released Rachel and yelled, "Look out, Lenny! We got trouble coming!"

Sarah could see Phil and Mike running toward them at top speed from the lodge.

"He's as big as a goddamn tree," Lenny said.

Lenny released Sarah, and she ran over to Rachel's side.

Taking the initiative, Lenny went to greet the would-be rescuers. He put out his hand to Mike, but Mike turned it away.

"I was showing your girlfriends here the fine deer we shot today," Lenny said.

Mike was staring at Lenny as if he were going to take a punch at him any second.

"Was he bothering you?" Phil asked Sarah.

Sarah didn't want a fight—the whole incident seemed more stupid and embarrassing than threatening—and she said no.

Lenny smiled with a toothy grin.

"That's what I was telling you," he said.

Mike continued to glare at Lenny; then he finally turned to the others and said, "Pick up your gear and let's go inside."

Sarah was greatly relieved. The last thing she wanted was to be the cause of a disturbance.

"I wish I had been here to take care of those assholes," Phil said in a threatening voice.

"It was no big deal," Sarah said.

"I think it was."

"Then I'm glad you weren't here."

As if Lenny had suddenly caught fire, he let out with a holler and grabbed his friend's arm, and the two of them ran toward the restaurant.

"We should have kicked their asses in," Phil said to Mike.

"Forget it."

Jim Wheatley, who had been silent throughout the discussion, spoke up for the first time. His voice sounded shaky.

"They weren't going to hurt anyone," he said.

"You sure as hell weren't going to stop them," Rachel said.

"I was trying to defuse the situation."

"You were trying to save your ass," Rachel said.

Jim didn't answer. He picked up his backpack and headed toward the lodge.

After the group had settled into their simple rooms, they met in the restaurant for their last civilized meal. Mike told them they should go to bed right after dinner, so they could get an early start the next morning.

"Why do we have to leave at six-thirty?" Rachel asked. "Ten o'clock sounds better to me."

"We'll be miles into the forest by ten o'clock," Mike said.

Rachel groaned.

20

The Pohick Bar and Grill was furnished with carved-up picnic tables and smelled of grease and beer and tobacco. Sarah saw only two other women in the restaurant. Both of them looked like alley cats caught in the rain. Their hair was long and ratty, their makeup was caked onto their bony features.

"Nice place," Jim said. "Real haute cuisine."

"Sometimes Mike and I find good food in these out of the way restaurants," Dianne said.

"And sometimes not so excellent," Mike added.

Phil pointed to the bar where Lenny and Bill were seated.

"It's our two friends from outside," he said.

"They won't come near us."

The hikers found an empty table and sat down.

"Can you believe all the people in this dive?" Jim said. "I guess there's not much to do around here but drink and count the toes you've lost to frostbite."

Mike stood up and waved across the room to a bald-headed man behind the counter.

"That's Bob Harwood," Mike said. "He's the one I met during that hunting trip in Pennsylvania last year."

Harwood came over to the table and greeted Mike like an old friend. Sarah was amazed at all the tattoos on his arms.

"Did you have any trouble finding us?" Harwood asked.

"No problem at all. Your directions were perfect."

As Mike introduced everyone, Sarah thought their host acted awfully cool toward the women.

"What's the special?" Mike asked.

"Pan-fried northern pike and cottage fries," he said in a booming voice. "Darn good, too."

"Then we'll all have the special," Mike said, getting the nod from the others. "And bring us some of those corn-bread patties you made on the hunting trip."

Dianne leaned over to Sarah.

"Mike really likes that guy. They had a great time hunting last year."

"Did you go with him?"

"I enjoy hiking, but killing animals leaves me cold."

"I know what you mean."

To Sarah, Bob Harwood looked like a kindergartner the way he clutched the pencil as he wrote down the order. Then he slipped the pencil behind his ear.

"Are you taking the trail I told you about?" he asked Mike.

"That's why we're here."

Harwood glanced at the women.

"I thought you were coming with your friends from work," he said.

"I did."

"I thought they'd all be men."

"Phil's a man," Rachel interrupted, "and Jim's pretty close to one."

"Does it make any difference?" Mike asked Harwood.

"Myself, I don't go into the back country with women. But it's your business."

"I'll take good care of them," Mike said.

"How long do you think it will take us to hike the trail?" Phil asked Harwood.

"With women along, I don't know."

"We're giving ourselves five days," Mike said.

"That might be about right."

"How's the weather?" Mike asked.

"It's been pretty cold, but by the way the fish are biting, I'd say you got warmer weather coming . . . good trail weather."

"Can you really tell what the weather will be like by how the fish bite?" Sarah asked.

"The fish bite on different moons. It's the moon that tells you what the weather will be."

"I don't believe it," Rachel said. "It sounds like predicting the snowfall by the length of hair on woolly worms."

"That's how you do it, ma'am," Harwood said. "How else would you know?"

"By watching TV."

Someone at the bar shouted for a drink, and Harwood left. As soon as he was gone, Phil turned to Mike and said, "I'd hate to run into him in an alley."

"Bob can take care of himself, that's for sure."

"I think he's a jerk," Rachel said.

"Harwood knows more about life than you ever will," Phil said. "People who live in the country aren't as stupid as you think."

"If you get turned on by muscles, that's fine. But don't expect me to climb on board."

"It's not only the muscles I admire. It's his knowledge about the wilderness."

"Do you think knowing how to track deer shit through the woods is going to help you make it in New York?"

"Harwood isn't a philosopher," Mike said, "but I bet you'd call on him before your New York friends if your life was in danger."

"I still think he's a dinosaur."

"I find him interesting myself," Dianne said.

"Harwood lost his wife a few years ago," Mike said. "It really put him through a meat grinder."

The conversation ended when Harwood returned to the table.

As Sarah watched the hulking man throw down the place settings, she was struck by how primitive everything was here. The men were loud and coarse, the lodge rough-hewn, everything bare and hard.

It seemed like strength and size were the only measures of things, and for the first time Sarah felt threatened.

When Harwood brought over the platters of steaming food, everyone dug right in. The pike was flaky white meat, sweet as spring water, and the cornbread patties were moist and savory.

"Dianne tried to make this cornbread, but it didn't come out the same," Mike said. "Even the dog wouldn't eat it."

Dianne kicked his leg under the table.

Sarah was a light eater—Phil called her picky—but tonight she loaded up on the food and mopped the sauce from her plate with the cornbread.

"I've never seen you eat so much," Phil said.

"I know. I feel like a pig."

"We might as well fill up," Dianne said. "From now on, it will be freeze-dried and canned food."

The jukebox played a loud, whining country song, and Sarah listened as the men in the bar began to sing:

> You're my woman
> I'm your man
> Love me good
> And I'll always be true to you.

Later, Dianne went to get more cornbread, and, a few minutes after she left, Phil pointed toward the counter and said, "Hey Mike, you better take a look at that."

Lenny and Bill were talking to Dianne and blocking her

23

path. To Sarah, it didn't look like they were bothering her. Dianne even waved, so her friends would know she was okay.

Just then, Sarah felt the bench heave back as Mike Stove charged across the room.

"What the hell is he doing?" Rachel said.

The whole restaurant was hushed as Mike ordered Dianne to return to the table.

"Go stop him," Sarah told Phil.

"Hell, no."

"But they're going to fight."

"Mike can take care of himself."

"You want him to get in a fight, don't you?"

Phil didn't answer. He stood up to get a better view, then moved closer toward the bar.

Lenny was slurring his words as he tried to explain to Mike that he was only asking if Dianne needed help carrying the food.

Without warning, Mike knocked Lenny's can of beer to the floor, and for a moment everyone held their breath.

Lenny smiled and told his friend, Bill, to wait out in the truck for him. Bill winked, then left. As soon as his friend was gone, Lenny reached down for the can of beer, then rocketed his fist up from the floor, snapping Mike's head back so hard that Sarah could see blood shoot across the counter.

As if a firecracker had gone off underneath the seats, every man in the bar jumped up and moved closer for a better view. They crowded around as Mike recovered and took his first glancing swing at Lenny.

"Kill the bastard!" Phil screamed.

Mike's lips were red with blood as he socked Lenny in the eye, sending him backward against the bar.

Everyone was egging the fighters on as Sarah stood up on the bench and craned her neck above the crowd. Though Mike had the height advantage, it looked to Sarah as if Lenny was getting the upper hand in the fight. Each time Mike scored with a punch, Lenny would get in a fast flurry, and he had soon opened up Mike's eye.

Both men were spitting blood.

Caught up in the excitement, Sarah began to root for Mike, her voice cracking with emotion. Dianne was jabbing her fists in the air as she watched her husband do battle.

The fight almost ended when Lenny kicked Mike in the groin. Mike bellowed and instantly doubled up, but, when Lenny came in to finish him off, Mike grabbed his head by the ears and drove Lenny's face into his knee. Lenny wilted to the floor, and, when he finally dragged himself back to his feet, his eyes were glazed.

"Finish him off!" Phil yelled.

Sarah screamed until her voice became hoarse. Her cheeks were flushed with excitement.

To get a better view, she stood up on the picnic table.

At that moment, Bill came back into the restaurant and stood at the door.

He was holding a shotgun.

Sarah tried to get Mike's attention, but her voice was drowned out by all the noise. She grabbed a stranger's shoulder and pointed wildly toward the door, but then she noticed Bob Harwood pull a shotgun out from under the bar and hold it high so that Bill had a clear line of sight.

The hunter's face turned red, and he broke into a grin as he rested his gun on the floor.

The fight continued with Mike and Lenny moving closer to Sarah's table—so close that she could hear each cracking punch, and she could hear the men snorting and grunting.

Mike took a quick step forward and smacked Lenny square in the jaw. Lenny fell backward on top of the table where Sarah was standing.

He rolled over on the dishes and reached for a knife, but Sarah stomped on his hand with her boot heel and kept stomping until he let go of the knife.

Mike lunged forward and pulled Lenny off the table, wrenching his arm up his back until Sarah thought it would pop out like a drumstick.

Lenny hollered as Mike dragged him by the scruff to the front of the restaurant and sent him sprawling headfirst into the door. Lenny slumped to the floor unconscious.

The restaurant exploded in cheers. Dianne ran over to Mike and jumped into his arms.

Mike craned his neck above the crowd and picked out Sarah. Then he waded through the back-slappers and lifted Sarah off the picnic table.

He gave her a quick kiss, then set her on the floor.

"I owe you one," he said.

The other hikers were all gathered around him now, and Phil grabbed a mug of beer from the table.

"Here's to Mike!" he shouted.

Again the restaurant broke into loud applause.

Meanwhile, Bill went over to Lenny and dragged his friend out the main door.

Sarah felt light-headed as the excitement began to subside and Mike and Phil recounted all the details of the fight. For the first time on the trip, Sarah felt close ties being forged among the group. They were no longer just acquaintances.

As Dianne cleaned Mike's wounds, Mike kept staring at Sarah with an appreciative smile. It was like the smile she remembered her brother, Jason, sharing with the guys on his little league team after a tough game.

It was like being a hero.

Later, after the hikers returned to their tiny rooms, Sarah was still bubbling with energy.

Phil wanted to go right to sleep, but Sarah had something else in mind.

"I feel like I was mugged," Phil said when the love-making was over.

"You loved it," Sarah said.

She kissed his chest, then rolled over on her back. They snuggled together under the heavy wool blankets and soon fell asleep.

Day Two

At exactly six A.M., Mike Stove banged on the door and yelled for Phil and Sarah to rise and shine. Sarah felt drugged with sleep, and both she and Phil lingered in bed for a while.

Then Phil rolled over and began to tickle Sarah's ribs.

"Stop it!" she cried as she squirmed to the edge of the bed and popped out from under the covers. Naked as a baby, she danced across the icy floor and raced to put on her clothes. Phil sat in bed laughing until Sarah came over and ripped the covers off.

"Jesus, it's cold!" he yelled. He tried to pull back the blankets, but Sarah held on to them.

Phil soon gave up and got out of bed, slapping his sides as he searched for his underwear.

When they were dressed they joined the other hikers in the restaurant, where Bob Harwood was already frying up a skillet of sausage.

"Doesn't he ever sleep?" Rachel asked.

"I think he sleeps after breakfast," Mike said. "But he's a hard worker. There's no doubt about that."

Mike's face showed the beating he had taken the night before. His jaw was swollen out of shape, his lip was split, and there was a black mouse under one eye.

Sarah was amazed that he was in such high spirits. In fact, Jim Wheatley seemed worse off. His face was pasty white, and Sarah guessed he had been drinking after everyone else went to their rooms.

"Are you ready for the trail?" Mike asked Rachel.

"I'm ready to go back to bed," Rachel said. She hid herself behind her mug of coffee.

Sarah watched Bob Harwood go over to the stove at the far end of the room and throw on more wood. He slammed

27

the iron door shut, then turned down the damper on the stove pipe and closed the draft at the bottom.

Sarah could feel the dry heat radiating throughout the room. She brightened up when Harwood brought her a steaming mug of coffee.

"How do you think I did last night?" Mike asked Harwood.

"You were lucky he was drunk."

"He was lucky I was tired," Mike said.

"I know Lenny Sours pretty well," Harwood said. "He bit the nose off of some trucker in here last week."

"He sure did a number on me."

Both men laughed, though Sarah could hardly understand why.

Sarah lit up a cigarette and noticed Phil giving her a disapproving glare.

"When you lose that spare tire, then I'll stop smoking," she said.

As the group ate a hearty breakfast, Bob Harwood kept pouring the coffee and refilling the platters with flapjacks. The smell of the food and the wood fire wakened Sarah's appetite. She ate six pancakes and four sausage links. When Phil left a couple pancakes on his plate, she ate those, too.

Dianne complained that the bed she had slept in the previous night had sagged, and she had a slight backache.

"You have to go easier on that wife of yours," Rachel told Mike. "Let her get on top sometimes."

When breakfast was over, Mike drew a rough sketch of the trail and explained the route. To Sarah, the map looked like the right side of a circle with an arrow shooting horizontally through it. The arrow turned out to be a river.

"We'll take three days to get around to the top and two days straight back," Mike said.

"I hope you have something better than this to guide us," Phil said.

"Harwood gave me a contour map."

Later the hikers assembled in the lobby, where there was an array of game trophies, including the head of a bear.

"You didn't get that from around here, did you?" Sarah asked Harwood.

"Sure did. Not more than five miles."

28

Dianne laughed.

"Don't worry," she said. "They're little black bears, not grizzlies. They won't bother you if you hang up your food in the trees at night."

"I thought the bears would be hibernating now," Phil said.

"A hungry bear will always go on the prowl," Mike said. "Besides, it's still early in the season."

"I don't even want to be on the same ground as a bear," Sarah said, "unless it's behind bars."

Mike thanked Harwood for the trail map and his hospitality.

"We'll see you when we get back," Mike said.

"I don't think so," Harwood said. "I'm taking off for a couple of weeks."

"Then I'll write to you soon. Maybe we can get another hunting trip going."

"Like the last one?" Harwood said with a smile.

"That's right. Maybe even better."

When Harwood was gone, Phil helped Sarah on with her backpack. She let out a tiny cry as the weight settled onto her shoulders.

"What was that for?" Phil asked.

"There's something wrong with the straps."

Phil checked them out.

"There's nothing wrong," he said.

"I wouldn't lie about it."

"Let's try the hip belt, and see what that does."

Phil clipped the belt onto the pack frame, then pulled it tight.

"Not so hard!" Sarah said.

"Don't be a baby."

Sarah drooped her shoulders so that more of the weight would fall on the hip belt, but it didn't help much.

"I've taken a few things out of the pack," Phil said. "If you want me to take more, I will."

"I didn't ask you to do that."

"I know you didn't. I was just trying to be nice."

"I'm not helpless, Phil. I know you like to think I am, but I'm not."

"I guess you woke up a little too early this morning."

"Just leave me alone, all right?"

Mike went back to the van. When he returned he was carrying a walking stick, and under his arm there was a shotgun inside a case.

"What's that for?" Sarah asked.

"I might want to do some hunting."

"I don't really care much for hunting," Sarah said.

"Then don't hunt."

Mike tied the shotgun onto the back of his pack; then, when everyone was ready, he led them down the front steps of the lodge, through the gravel lot, and into the meadow.

Across the open field Sarah could see the forest shrouded in fog. There was no sun, no sky, only a gray mist hovering in the tree tops.

"Harwood's fish aren't very good weathermen," Rachel said.

"That haze will burn off soon," Dianne said. "A hundred feet up there's blue skies."

The hikers were walking single file with their backpacks towering above their heads. They were leaning forward with the change in center of gravity.

Since Sarah couldn't remember its having rained the previous night, she was surprised to find the ground soaked. The tall grass was wet and sticky, and her weather-proofed boots were beaded up with water.

"Did it rain last night?" she asked Dianne.

"No, there's just a lot of dew in the morning because of the sharp temperature change. When you wake up tomorrow, your tent will be dripping with water."

The ground was stony and uneven, and Sarah was afraid she was going to fall. With the heavy pack on her back, she could have easily twisted her ankle and ruined the whole trip.

She kept looking at Dianne and Rachel, who were consistently hiking faster than she was. Everyone, including Phil, seemed to be having an easier time.

When they reached the treeline, Sarah thought she deserved a rest, so she was disappointed when Mike headed straight into the forest.

She caught her breath, then followed the others in.

"How's it going?" Phil asked after they had been walking a few minutes.

"I hate it."

"It gets better when you catch your stride," Dianne said. "It takes a while to warm up."

Already the load of the pack was pulling at her shoulder muscles. It felt like a huge hand pinching the back of her neck. Sarah put her fingers under the straps to lift off some of the weight, but it was little use.

Sarah asked Dianne how long it would take to reach the trail, and she was surprised when she learned they were already on it.

To Sarah, it was nothing but tall grass, stone, and underbrush—indistinguishable from any other part of the forest.

"This isn't like hiking at home," Mike said. "There aren't any paved trails out here."

Mike always made a sharp distinction between weekend "campers" with their Coleman stoves and RV's, and what he called "real backpackers."

"You have to go farther and farther away to get rid of the assholes," he said.

Sarah couldn't see very far into the forest because of the thick fog that was like an impenetrable bubble all around them. When she turned around and looked behind her, the trail disappeared into the gray mist.

The evergreen trees continued to be much smaller than Sarah had expected, and they were crowded so closely together that at times the hikers had to brush against the branches.

Phil explained that much of the forest had been cut down by the lumber companies not long ago.

"How do you know so much about it?" Sarah asked him.

"Mike told me. You can learn a lot from him, Sarah."

She looked at the front of the column of hikers and saw Mike attacking the trail as he had attacked the highway the day before.

After half an hour of walking, Sarah swore that the shoulder straps were cutting off her circulation. Her arms felt like they were asleep.

She gained some relief by slumping her shoulders so that more weight fell on her hips, but then her right thigh began to pinch.

She was constantly choosing between two kinds of pain —neither one particularly more pleasant than the other.

31

The final ten minutes before the hourly break went as slowly as an afternoon at work in the insurance office. Sarah felt like cheering when the word finally came to halt.

Before the others had their straps off, Sarah dumped her pack on the trail and sat on the ground. She lit up a cigarette and coughed a few times before catching her breath.

Jim Wheatley came over and sat down beside her, his face pale green.

"I don't know about you," he said, "but I'm not having fun."

"I thought you looked pretty good out there," Sarah said.

"That's because you didn't see me throw up a few minutes ago."

"Don't even say that word."

Jim burped, and Sarah could smell the gin on his breath. His fine brown hair was wet with perspiration.

"I noticed that Phil is keeping up with Mike," Jim said.

"It's ridiculous how competitive he is at his age."

"I don't know. If it makes him feel better, who am I to throw stones?"

"If Phil wants to butt horns with Mike, that's okay, but I don't like it when he turns around and takes a few licks at me."

"You're a lot easier to lick."

"I know."

While Sarah and Jim were talking, Mike Stove came over and told them that they were wearing too many clothes.

"The trick is to dress up and peel down with your body temperature," Mike said. "You don't want to get hypothermia."

"If that's a ticket home, I'll take it," Jim said.

"Hypothermia isn't a joke. It can kill you."

"Excuse me for being so irreverent."

As if he were talking to school children, Mike gave Sarah and Jim a short lecture on the dangers of hypothermia. He told them about the tiredness and dampness, the chills and hallucinations. Finally, he told them that the best way to save someone in the advanced stages of hypothermia was to put him in a sleeping bag and crawl inside to warm him. In less severe cases, the best cure was food and constant movement to warm the core of the body.

"I once heard about an Indian who saved a friend by sticking him inside the carcass of a deer," Mike said.

"I think I'd rather die," Sarah said.

"In any case, take off those parkas. You don't need them."

"Yes, sir!" Jim said with a snappy salute.

"You'd better take what I say more seriously," Mike said. "This isn't the insurance office. You can get hurt out here."

When Mike left, Jim turned to Sarah and said, "Does it sound like he's getting bossier?"

"Mike's always been a little bossy."

"I know, but I think it's getting worse."

Jim stood up and excused himself. He said he wanted to get some water, but Sarah saw him pull a flask out of his backpack and take it behind a tree. While he was gone, Rachel came over and joked about Jim's getting sick.

"By the way," Sarah said, "how do you go to the bathroom out here?"

"You just head off into the woods and do it," Rachel said. "You'd better hurry up though. Mike's getting ready to leave."

Sarah dragged herself off the ground and rubbed her sore leg.

"Tell Mike to go on without me. I'll catch up."

"I'll tell him, but I'm going to wait for you."

Sarah got her toilet paper from the side pocket of her backpack and walked into the fir trees until she couldn't see anyone. She looked around for a good spot that didn't look dirty, and finally decided on a small area that was covered with a blanket of pine needles.

Everything felt wet and sticky. If there had been any way she could have held off, she would have done it. But there was no way.

She dropped her pants and pulled down her long underwear. When she bent over, she lost her balance and fell to the ground. Pine needles stuck to her backside.

"Dammit," Sarah said. "I could be home sitting on a padded toilet seat."

The next time she squatted, she held on to a tree limb so she wouldn't fall back, but she still trickled on her leg and pants, and her toilet paper fell to the ground and rolled out down the hill.

33

When she was finished, Sarah quickly pulled up her pants and ran back to join the others. Everyone had gone on without her except for Rachel.

"How did it work out?" Rachel asked.

"I'm not going to the bathroom the rest of the trip."

"Lots of luck."

Rachel helped her on with her pack, and they walked off to catch up with the others.

"Do your shoulder straps hurt?" Sarah asked.

"No."

"Mine do. I told Phil about it, but he says there's nothing wrong with them."

"Then tell him to carry your pack awhile and see for himself."

"I wish I had thought of that."

"You have to get a little tougher with these bastards out here."

"What do you mean?"

"Being in the woods turns men into bullies. They think they're boy scouts again, running around summer camp, playing with their peckers."

Sarah laughed.

"It's true. Believe me."

"I'll have to remember that."

Later that morning the haze burned off and opened up a cloudless blue sky. The sun was bright, but to Sarah it looked cold and distant.

As the hikers made their way up a slow rise in the trail, Sarah had the feeling that the land was working against her. Defying the law of gravity, the hills went constantly up without ever coming down again. Whenever Sarah thought they had finally reached the top of a rise, the trail would switch back and climb again.

The air was crisp and cold, but Sarah was sweating. She unbuttoned the top of her shirt and let the breeze reach her chest.

In spite of her best effort, Sarah could tell that the rest of the group was slowly pulling ahead, and she knew she was holding Rachel back.

"Catch up with the others," she told Rachel.

"I'm in no rush."

34

."Go ahead. I'll be okay."

"Are you sure?"

"I want to walk alone for a while."

"Good enough."

With an ease that made Sarah envious, Rachel quickly hiked back up to the others.

During the next couple of hours, the routine was the same—Sarah would fall behind, then catch up during the rest breaks.

"Can't you walk any faster?" Phil asked as she straggled in shortly before the rest break was over.

"I'm surprised I've made it at all," Sarah said. "These shoulder straps are killing me."

"Don't blame it on the straps. Mike and I bought you the best pack they make."

"Then it must be perfect. I'm sure that I'm imagining the pain."

"You don't see anyone else complaining."

"Oh, shut up."

Sarah walked quickly away.

Although she walked alone most of the time, sometimes a member of the group would drop back to visit her. Sarah hated the visits because they made her feel like the runt of the litter.

Mike Stove's sick calls were particularly unpleasant and embarrassing.

"Do you want me to slow up more?" he asked.

"I'll be okay."

"I think I'll slow up anyway."

"If you're going to do it anyway, then why ask?"

Phil also dropped back to check on her from time to time.

"How are you holding up?"

"Just fine. Leave me alone."

"I'm only trying to help."

"Then leave me alone."

Sarah could tell that Phil was struggling to keep up with Mike. His face was red, and the veins in his neck bulged.

"If you're not careful, you're going to have a heart attack," Sarah said. "You're puffing like an old blowfish."

"Heart attack?" Phil blustered. "Don't be an idiot."

The barb struck deep, and Sarah was pleased. Who said it wasn't fun to be mean?

"Besides," Phil said, "you're the one with the bad ticker."

"That's a cheap shot. There's nothing wrong with my heart, and you know it."

Ignoring her, Phil charged ahead, and Sarah listened to him huff and puff his way back to the front of the line.

Sarah continued to fall farther and farther behind until she could barely see the others. Sometimes Dianne would turn and wave to her, and Sarah would wave back to show she was okay.

During one of the rest breaks, Mike came over to her as she was sprawled out on her poncho.

"I told you it would be rough," he said.

"Not this rough. I thought it might be a little fun, too, and it isn't."

Sarah sat up Indian-style on the poncho.

"Would you believe I jogged every day for two months to get ready for this trip?"

"Phil didn't tell me."

"That's because he didn't know. I was scared to death I wouldn't be able to keep up with everyone, and now it's happening."

Mike laughed.

"You use different leg muscles when you jog," Mike said. "But it'll pay off."

"Even Phil's doing better than I am."

"Today he is, but he's working too hard. He won't have the long-term endurance that you do."

Sarah looked over at Phil, who was leaning against a tree with his head buried in his arms.

Meanwhile, Mike went over to the pack that Sarah had dropped in the middle of the trail.

"You ought to take better care of your gear," he said.

He unhooked the shock cord and removed Sarah's sleeping bag from the pack frame.

"What are you doing?" Sarah asked.

"I'm going to carry a few things for you."

After he had removed her sleeping bag from the pack frame, Mike took a few cans of food out, too.

"I wish you wouldn't do that," she told him.

"Don't get excited. I'm only trying to help you out."

"And if I told you I don't want your help, you'd think I'm a bitch, right?"

"That's right."

Mike carried the stolen goods to his own pack and stashed them inside. Then he looked back at Sarah and winked playfully.

Sarah knew that it was useless to argue.

"Let's go," Mike announced to the group when the break was over. "We're running behind."

Sarah picked up her pack and was trying to put it on when Phil came over unexpectedly to help her.

"Thanks," she said when the pack was on her shoulders.

Without a word said, he yanked the hip belt tightly around her waist and walked away.

"Asshole," Sarah muttered to herself.

For the next few miles, the only thought that sustained Sarah was the prospect of stopping a full hour at lunchtime.

She kept telling herself to walk by the count...keep up the rhythm...take her mind off the pain.

None of it worked.

As she lagged almost out of sight of the others, she began to hum to herself and pretend she was lying on a sandy beach in Florida with a golden-skinned man of fifty on her right and a large-shouldered boy of twenty on her left, both of them massaging her with suntan lotion.

Lost in her fantasy, she caught her boot under a stone and fell flat on her face. When she got up and brushed herself off, she looked far ahead where Phil was outdistancing Mike and charging full-steam up the side of the hill.

Sarah secretly hoped he would faint or do anything that would embarrass him in front of the others. As she pictured Phil on his hands and knees vomiting on the trail, a smile broke out on her sweaty face.

Sarah was so preoccupied with hiking that it took her a while to notice that the nature of the forest had changed drastically.

The pine trees now shot to the sky like gigantic supporting columns. Their long, bare shafts rose hundreds of feet and bloomed into conical heads of evergreen branches.

The floor of the forest became dark and rich. It smelled

37

musty, like rotting vegetation and damp soil. She could feel her boots sink into the spongy layer of pine needles. The ground seemed like it might collapse under her weight at any moment.

Not long after they entered the first growth forest, they came to a large pond that was frozen clean and smooth. It sparkled in the sunlight that broke through the circular opening in the trees. The overall darkness of the forest made the pond even brighter in comparison, and its beauty was enough to distract Sarah from her pain.

She looked ahead and could see her friends rounding the far end of the pond and moving beyond it into the forest. The thousands of branchless tree trunks separated them like iron bars. Soon the group disappeared as the trail switched back out of view.

Sarah stopped by the pond's edge and watched as a squirrel cautiously went out on the ice a few feet, then scurried back into the forest.

Sarah knew that if she could walk across the pond it would cut several hundred yards off the distance she would have to travel. She would catch up with the others in no time.

Frozen ponds were nothing new to Sarah. As a little girl, she had spent many hours on her father's shoulders as he skated across the bumpy ice in an old stone quarry. The quarry was used as a dumping site, so there were always tires and rusty barrels sticking out of the ice.

Skating in the quarry was considered dangerous, but Sarah always felt safe on her father's back as he raced at breakneck speed, the wind blowing through his hair.

"Go faster!" Sarah would scream.

Her father's legs seemed to explode with power each time he took a stride. Daringly, he would head straight for a barrel and leap over it, landing cleanly on the other side while Sarah clutched his back and giggled nervously.

Sarah always wanted to stay the entire day, but her father would grow tired and tell her it was time to go home.

The childhood memory faded as Sarah looked across the pond. She picked up a large stone from the shore and threw it out onto the ice. It bounced a few times and skidded to a stop.

The solid sound of the impact was reassuring.

Sarah cautiously tested the ice with her weight, stepping out a few yards and lightly jumping up and down.

It seemed fine.

Anxious to catch up with the others, Sarah headed for the other side of the pond, walking gingerly at first, but then picking up the pace as she became more confident. Her new hiking boots gripped the ice well.

When she reached the halfway mark, Sarah thought she was rather clever, and she was sure that Mike and Phil would be impressed by how quickly she had caught up.

She had just begun the final leg of the crossing when she heard the first crisp snap in the ice.

She stopped in her tracks and looked carefully all around, but could see nothing. She drew a deep breath, then walked softly a few steps farther, listening for any telltale signs. The other shore was so close now that Sarah quickened the pace, hoping to get the crossing over with as soon as possible.

When the second crack sounded through the still forest, it was entirely different from the first. It began as a crisp snap, but then it continued like the sound of a zipper being slowly opened, then opening faster and faster until Sarah turned and saw the crack racing straight for her feet as if the ice had targeted her for having dared to cross.

She began to run for the shoreline, screaming for help, when suddenly the ice heaved up on both sides of her like a trap door opening, and she plunged into the icy water.

She thrashed about like a gaffed fish, fighting for air, struggling to undo the shoulder straps. The pack was dragging her down. It felt like someone clutching stubbornly to her back.

Sarah stiffened up when the biting cold water soaked to her skin. The straps were stuck. The heavy pack dragged her slowly down to the bottom of the pond.

Her lungs burning for air, Sarah strained against the buckles until she finally pulled off the shoulder straps. She pushed off the bottom of the pond and swam for the surface, only to find herself entombed by ice.

But she could breathe. There was air on her face, and she was sucking it up in great volumes, bathing her lungs with the air's freshness. Then she realized that there was a narrow gap between the ice and the water level of the pond.

Treading water she could pin her face against the ice, and yes, she could breathe!

Her arms grew weak, her legs numb. She could hear herself panting for air as if there were a bucket over her head. Whenever something hit the surface, it made a sharp pinging sound. She could look up through the layer of ice and see the murky outline of the giant pine trees around the pond. It was like looking at them in a dream.

Sarah could feel a warm glow moving up her legs and into her thighs, and she was becoming so tired and numb that she felt like giving up.

But Sarah's body screamed for life even as her will faltered. The scream was raw and irrational; it couldn't be silenced.

She moved around under the ice, panting for air, searching for the escape hole. Suddenly she felt her feet sink into the mucky bottom of the pond. She could stand up now and rest. She no longer had to tread water.

Sarah screamed and beat her fist against the ice, and kept pounding until her arms went limp.

Suddenly she heard a loud crack, and soon the entire pond was cracking like lightning all around her.

As she looked up through the ice, she saw something dark. At first she thought a branch had fallen on the pond, but then she realized someone was standing above her.

It was Mike Stove!

Sarah began to beat her fist against the ice again.

"It's me!" she screamed. "Can't you see me?"

Mike got down on his knees and swirled his glove around on the ice. Then, as if seeing a figure jump out of an inkblot, his face lit up and he yelled for Sarah to stay put.

Mike left but returned a few seconds later, and Sarah could hear him chipping away at the ice with a hatchet. She covered her ears against the deafening sound as Mike broke through, knocking out larger and larger sections until he could reach down and grab hold of Sarah.

The next thing she knew she was being dragged up onto the ice. Mike was lying spreadeagle while Phil and Jim pulled him back from the hole by his legs. As soon as they were on safe ice, Mike stood up and lifted Sarah into his arms.

She tried to speak, but her teeth were chattering uncontrollably.

"Don't talk," Mike said. "I'll warm you up in no time."

His voice was strong and sure. In her confusion, Sarah imagined she was being held by her father.

A stiff breeze blew through the forest, and Mike carried Sarah into the shelter of the trees and shouted orders to the anxious hikers.

"Sleeping bags!" he yelled to Dianne. "Two of them!" Turning to Rachel, he said, "Start a fire and start it fast, and get Jim to help you."

Phil was standing rigid with shock.

"Get some hot coffee going!" Mike shouted.

The brisk command jolted him into action.

Dianne raced back with the sleeping bags and helped Mike strip off Sarah's wet clothes. They doubled up the bags, then Mike got inside with Sarah and hugged her tightly.

Jim and Rachel had piled up some kindling nearby but were having trouble getting the fire started because of the wind.

"Use balls of wax paper!" Mike shouted. "There's a roll in my pack."

Rachel got the paper and balled it up under the kindling. When she lit the fire this time, the wind blew it around, but the wax paper burned even harder.

Phil shoved a pan of water directly into the flames and looked nervously at Sarah as he waited for the steam to rise.

"Is she going to be all right?" he asked Mike.

"Just worry about the coffee!"

Mike hugged Sarah tightly, but even with all his strength he could not stop her violent shivering.

Jim and Rachel had the wood piled waist high now, and they continued to add more.

"That's enough," Mike told them. "We don't need a bonfire."

Mike put his lips close to Sarah's ear and said, "I've got it under control. You'll be fine."

The fire was crackling and spitting, heat billowing up into the trees, swaying the branches. Sarah stared at the flames as if they were life itself.

"The coffee's ready," Phil said as he rushed over with two mugs in his hands.

"One will do," Dianne said. She took one of the mugs and gave it to Mike. Mike lifted Sarah's head from the ground and told Sarah to drink.

She coughed up the first sip, but when she drank again she could feel the hot drink moving down her throat into her stomach.

As Sarah came back to life, she felt tingling all over her skin. The backs of her legs were stinging terribly.

Phil brought over more coffee and knelt down beside her on the ground.

His face was still pale.

"Next time you decide to go swimming," he said, "take me along."

Sarah reached out and held his hand.

As soon as she was able, Mike had Sarah dress in some of Rachel and Dianne's extra clothes; then he walked her around the area until she was completely warmed.

"How long was I under the ice?" she asked Mike. "It felt like forever."

"You would have been dead in twenty minutes," he said. "I'd guess you weren't under more than five."

"You're kidding."

"We ran back when we heard you scream. You were damn lucky we found you right away. And you were lucky the water level dropped after the pond froze."

As Sarah warmed herself by the fire, she apologized repeatedly for her stupidity.

"We all make mistakes the first time out," Dianne said. "The first time I went camping with Mike, I took a walk alone after dinner and ended up having the park rangers search for me."

While Sarah talked to Dianne, she noticed Mike and Phil move away for a private conference. When they returned, Mike looked at everyone and said, "As soon as Sarah's clothes are dry, we're returning to the lodge."

If Mike had thrown Sarah back into the icy pond, she couldn't have been more shocked.

"Why?" she said.

"I want you checked out by a doctor."

"That's crazy. I don't need a doctor."

Phil came over and put his arm around her and gave her a sympathetic hug.

42

"It's not your fault," he said in a soothing tone of voice. "Mike doesn't want to take any chances."

Sarah pushed Phil away and walked over to confront Mike.

"I want to keep going," she said.

"You're my responsibility here. I brought you on this trip, and I don't want anything to happen to you."

"That's my business, not yours."

Dianne went to Mike and held his hand.

"Why don't we keep going today? If Sarah doesn't feel well, we can turn back later."

"I'm worried about the heart problem she had."

"You're only using that as an excuse," Sarah said angrily.

"An excuse for what?"

"If Jim or Phil had fallen in the pond, we wouldn't be heading back, and you know it."

Phil told her she was making a fool of herself and to shut up and listen to Mike.

"Thanks for your support," Sarah said. "I'll remember that."

Mike argued that they would have to turn back even if Sarah didn't get sick.

"You've lost your backpack. You don't have any gear."

"She can wear my clothes," Rachel said.

"And your boots are soaked."

"She can wear the running shoes I brought," Dianne said. "She can tie her boots on Phil's pack and let them dry."

Mike was at a loss for words. He looked at the circle of women around him as if he were under attack.

"Show us what a nice guy you are," Dianne teased.

Mike looked around skeptically, then said in a gruff voice, "Let's eat lunch. If we're going ahead with this trip, we can't stand around here all day."

Sarah told Rachel and Dianne that she would take turns carrying their packs, so it would be fair to everyone. They agreed as long as Sarah walked the rest of the day without a pack. The next day they would switch off.

Sarah gave both women a hug. She felt very close to them. As for Phil, she hoped he would drop dead.

As if almost drowning had increased her appetite, Sarah

43

inhaled her lunch, quickly going through a pouch of freeze-dried spaghetti, a can of fruit, a health bar, and a full quart of lemonade.

After the meal, she lit up a smoke, but ground it in the dirt after a few puffs. The cigarettes had lost their flavor.

When it was time to go, Mike picked up his walking stick and led the group back to the trail. Phil tried to walk beside Sarah, but she dropped back away from him and linked up with Rachel.

"That's showing him," Rachel said. "Kick him in the ass once in a while."

"Is that what you do with Jim?"

"He wouldn't have it any other way."

It was far easier hiking without a pack, and even after two hours Sarah had not fallen behind. Her thigh still pinched a little, but her shoulders felt much better.

The back country was beautiful now that Sarah wasn't stabbed with pain. The tall pines, with their sparse and scraggly lower branches, supported an evergreen canopy overhead.

Except for the sounds of the group hiking on the overgrown path, there was an all-pervading stillness in the forest, broken only by the occasional call of a jay.

It was stupid to have gone on the trip, Sarah thought, but now that she was here, she was damn well going to finish it.

"Tell me about your ex-husband," Rachel said as they climbed over a fallen tree across the path.

"I don't like to talk about it."

"You can learn a lot from reading the bones."

"Whenever I think about it, I get depressed. And to tell you the truth, I'm embarrassed by how stupid I was."

"I hope you don't think you're the first woman to be fucked over by a man," Rachel said.

"I know I'm not, but it doesn't make it any easier to be in a crowd."

"Marriage never worked for me either."

"What about your marriage with Jim?"

"It's not really a marriage. It's more of an arrangement."

"I don't follow."

"We have an open marriage."

"Does it work?"

"For me it does."

"And what about Jim?"

"He knows I won't stay with him any other way, so he puts up with it. He gets what he wants out of the relationship."

"I'm sick of relationships," Sarah said. "They're too complicated."

"They're not so bad. I've found that there are really only two kinds of men in the world."

"That would make things easier for me. What are they?"

"Winners and losers," Rachel said.

"I already know that," Sarah said. "The problem is how to find the winners."

"That's just the point. You don't always want a winner. Winners have to take complete control of their women. Losers are just the opposite. You can do anything to them, and they'll stick to you like cow shit."

"That's a hell of a choice," Sarah said.

"It's true though. Take your ex-husband, for example. I bet he was a winner."

"I thought he was."

"He always had his way with you, didn't he?"

"Yes."

"And he was terribly ambitious."

"All he lived and breathed was medical school."

"And he was great-looking and terrific in bed."

"He wasn't bad."

"And now he's finished med school, has a rich practice going, and spends all his time at medical seminars in Saint Croix."

"It sounds awfully simple when you put it that way, but you're not far off the mark."

"And he treated you miserably, didn't he?"

"He took me for a ride through med school. I typed his papers, washed his clothes, took care of everything. I even gave up a chance to finish college, so I could support him while he was in school."

"And then he left you."

"I told him to get out, but he was going to leave me anyway."

45

"Men are shits, Sarah. Remember that. Winners or losers, they're all shits."

"Some are shittier than others."

"How are things with Phil?"

"Sometimes it works; sometimes it doesn't."

"You want some advice?"

"Okay."

"Don't marry him. Let him live with you, but don't marry him. Be ready to bail out at any time."

"I haven't made any commitments."

"You're being smart."

"Getting burned makes you that way."

As they continued to walk together, Sarah began to admire Rachel's no-nonsense view of male-female relationships. Rachel was far more realistic about finding happiness than Sarah was.

"If you don't expect much from men," Rachel said, "you'll be surprised by how well they measure up."

Rachel's advice was for Sarah to start getting tougher with Phil to see how he would react.

"You've got to stop trying to relate to him and learn how to deal with him instead," she said.

But Sarah wasn't sure whether she wanted to learn how to deal with Phil. She knew that relationships demanded work, but how much energy did you have to invest before it simply wasn't worth it anymore?

It was true that Phil had saved her during a crisis in her life, she thought, but was that any basis for a relationship?

The longer it dragged on, the harder it would be to cut it off. The conclusion was unavoidable: when Sarah got back to New York, she would do the hard and courageous thing . . . the right thing.

She was more convinced now than she had been the other dozen times she had arrived at the same conclusion. Once she had even gone through with it. She cried. Phil cried. The separation lasted one week to the day, and they both swore they would never hurt each other that way again.

The entire week Sarah had felt angry with herself for feeling lonely. She felt lonely when she was with her women friends and lonely when she went out with another man. Jim Wheatley told her that it was because she was in love with Phil, but she knew that wasn't the reason.

46

If anything, she was "in habit" with Phil, not "in love."

If he were only a tiny bit worse, it would be so easy to give him the boot . . . permanently.

But he wasn't that bad. He was probably as good as most men.

If only there were some way to reform him.

During the late afternoon, Sarah talked Rachel into letting her carry the backpack, and she was surprised to find that the shoulder straps didn't hurt.

It confirmed her belief that the other pack had been defective, no matter what Phil said.

As the hikers followed a small creek that ran through the hollow, Sarah noticed how fast the light was receding, and, along with it, how sharply the temperature had dropped.

"This is where we'll stop for the night," Mike announced. He pointed out a clearing not very far from the creek, where he told them to pitch their tents.

Sarah was amazed at how energetic she felt, despite the day's hike and the incident at the pond. Oddly enough, she felt better than she had when they first started off.

"Can you help me with the tent?" Phil asked as he unrolled it on the ground.

It was the first time they had spoken in hours.

"Okay," Sarah said coolly.

As they pitched the tent, it was clear that Phil was trying to make peace without having to apologize. He went out of his way to explain each step of the procedure, and, when Sarah made a dumb mistake or got in the way, he would smile and tell her it was okay.

Sarah didn't say a word the entire time so that Phil would learn the price of her forgiveness.

Mike and Dianne erected their free-standing tent first, and Sarah and Phil weren't far behind. They entertained themselves for a while by watching the comical antics of the Wheatleys. Rachel ordered Jim around like a drill sergeant while he fumbled with the metal frame and stopped to take a drink every few minutes. At one point Rachel had the tent up, but Jim tripped on it, and the tent collapsed.

"I'm going to shove the poles up your ass next time," Rachel said.

47

Dianne and Sarah jumped in to help, and soon the Wheatleys' tent was standing alongside the others.

Mike and Phil went off into the woods to make a biffy; then later they returned and started a fire.

Sarah and Dianne volunteered to fill up the five-gallon water jug down at the creek.

"You better wear a jacket," Dianne said. "It's getting awfully chilly."

"I lost mine at the pond."

Dianne reached for a parka that was hanging over a tree limb next to her tent.

"Here," she said, handing the jacket to Sarah. "Wear Mike's."

The sleeves were much longer than Sarah's arms, and the parka came down past her knees. When she threw the floppy hood over her head, the jacket looked like it had swallowed her up.

They took the five-gallon plastic jug and several canteens to the edge of the creek and walked downstream about fifty yards to some rocks that made a good place to fill the jugs.

They leaned over, past the fringe of ice and into the rushing part of the creek, and dipped the canteens in the water.

"I really appreciate you standing up for me," Sarah said.

"You mean back by the pond?"

"Yes. I hope I didn't put you in a bad position with Mike."

"Not at all. If Phil hadn't mentioned your heart problem, I don't think Mike would have ever thought about going back."

Sarah screwed on the top of a canteen and found a pool in the creek where she could fill up the large jug.

"To tell you the truth," Dianne said, "Mike admires you for wanting to go on."

"He does? I thought he was angry with me."

"That's the way Mike is. But he told me he thought you had guts."

"I wish he had told me himself."

"Mike doesn't operate that way," Dianne said.

Sarah's right hand became numb from the icy water, so she switched to the left. It was hard to fill the jug in such a shallow creek.

"Don't let Mike hurt your feelings," Dianne continued. "He doesn't always think as much as he should, and sometimes he's awfully insensitive."

"I think all men are."

"You take the good with the bad."

When the jug was as full as they could get it, Dianne and Sarah lifted it from the water. They slung the canteens over their shoulders, then carried the jug between them. It was a heavy load, and it was good to be sharing it.

The forest was completely dark now. They could see the large fire going not far from the tents, and they could see Mike Stove cutting logs with a bow saw.

"I don't understand why you don't get as frustrated by Mike as I do by Phil," Sarah asked.

"I hate to give advice about relationships. I just do what works."

"But that's the point," Sarah said. "Your relationship works, and mine never seem to."

"I think the worst thing you can do is try to change a person," Dianne said. "I figure that Mike isn't going to change me, and I'm not going to change him."

"But what if you're unhappy?"

"Everyone's a little unhappy."

"I mean very unhappy. The kind of unhappy where you don't want to get up in the morning."

"Then you get out of the relationship . . . like you did with Gary."

Dianne stopped walking.

"Not everything pleases me about Mike," she said, "but overall it's good, and we have a great time together. I put up with the other things and try not to think about them."

Sarah smiled warmly.

"Thanks again for speaking up for me," she said.

"I'm glad you decided to come on the trip."

They picked up the heavy jug and walked the rest of the way to camp.

When they arrived at the tents, Mike told everyone to put away the freeze-dried food and the cans and the reconstituted drinks and get ready for a surprise.

He dipped into his backpack and pulled out six prime steaks, each one as big as his hand.

"I thought you were a purist," Jim said.

"You have to promise not to tell anyone about this," Mike said. "I wanted to celebrate your first night in the back country."

Dianne went to her backpack and took out a plastic jug of red wine.

"And here's my contribution," she said.

"I don't believe you guys carried all that weight," Phil said, astonished. "And I thought I was keeping up with you."

"You were," Mike said.

"But I wasn't carrying a side of beef with me."

The freeze-dried food was quickly packed away, and Mike demonstrated how to make a grill out of green branches so it wouldn't burn in the fire.

Phil and Jim picked up a fallen tree and placed it down near the fire so everyone could sit on it.

"This isn't as bad as I thought it would be," Jim said.

When the steaks were nicely charred, Mike passed them around, and the group lost no time getting down to serious eating.

"Perfect," Rachel said. "I like my steaks almost raw."

Near the end of the meal, Jim stood up and announced that he too had brought a little surprise.

Everyone watched as he went to his backpack and took out a box of cigars and a large flask.

"What's a steak dinner without brandy?" he said.

"I think I'll skip the cigars," Sarah said, "but the brandy sounds good."

For a long time after the meal, the group sat around the campfire sipping brandy, talking, and staring into the black sky with its piercing stars and a moon that looked like a hungry animal had taken a bite out of it.

"This is really nice," Sarah said as she snuggled closer to Phil, still wearing Mike's floppy jacket.

Phil kissed her. Then he apologized for not sticking up for her back at the pond.

Sarah was greatly surprised. It wasn't Phil's style to apologize for anything.

"Do you know any ghost stories?" Jim asked Mike.

"Ghost stories are for girl scouts," he said. "But I know something about the Indians in the area."

"Indians are vastly overrated," Rachel said. "They're big on nature, but they treat their women like cattle."

50

"Have you read anything about them?" Mike asked.

"I dated one for a year."

"Maybe he was just a bad egg."

"All his Indian friends were bad eggs, too. They'd get naked inside a smoke-filled tent and do dope and find religion. No women allowed of course."

Dianne served everyone coffee from a blackened enamel pot while Mike stirred the fire with a branch. The burning logs rolled over, shooting sparks into the night air.

"If you don't want to hear about Indians," Mike said, "then maybe I can teach you how to find your way around the wilderness."

"I think I'll pass up the lecture," Jim said.

"Let's humor Mike," Phil said. "It makes him feel good to show us how clever he is."

"Forget it," Mike said.

"They're only kidding you," Dianne said. "Go ahead."

"Yeah," Jim said. "We're only kidding."

"Then wipe the smirk off your face."

"Done," Jim said, tightening his lips.

Mike stood in front of the hikers, who were sitting lined up along the log like proper students.

"The first thing you need to learn," he began, "is how to walk in a straight line."

"You'd better listen closely to this," Rachel said to Jim. "You can use it the next time the troopers pull you over."

"Be quiet. This is serious."

"People tend to walk in circles when they don't have anything to go by," Mike continued.

"Is there an allegory in there someplace?" Jim asked.

Everyone told Jim to shut up.

"Like I was saying, people tend to walk in circles, so it's important to line up markers ahead of you."

"Why can't you simply walk by the sun?" Sarah asked.

"That's fine if there is any sun, and even then it's not very accurate."

"I'd never go anywhere alone unless I had a compass," Phil said.

"But if you didn't have one, you could still get out of a jam by lining up trees ahead of you. Then all you have to do is make sure you sight up another tree when you arrive at the first."

51

."Show them that trick with the wristwatch," Dianne said.

"There isn't any sunlight."

"Use the fire. We can pretend it's the sun."

Mike broke a twig off a branch and held his forearm out toward the fire.

"If you don't have a compass, you can make one with your watch," he said. "You place the twig along the outside of the watch and get the shadow from the sun to line up with the hour hand. Then all you have to do is run an imaginary line between the hour and twelve o'clock, and bingo, you have true south."

"Wouldn't it be a lot easier to call AAA?" Jim said. "They give you a nice little trip-tick, and it's free if you're a member."

"Can't you be serious about anything?" Mike said.

"I used to be serious about death and screwing," Jim said, "but the more I thought about them, the more ludicrous they became."

"I can vouch that his screwing is ludicrous," Rachel said.

In an attempt to change the subject, Dianne asked Mike to explain to the hikers how to collect water when there wasn't any around.

Rachel stood up and brushed off her backside.

"I think I'm going to turn in," she said with a yawn.

"Don't you want to find out how to do it?" Mike said.

"Believe me, honey. I already know how to do it."

Jim, Sarah, and Phil took Rachel's cue and said that they too were going to bed.

"Wait a moment," Mike said.

He unbuckled the hunting knife he carried on his belt and brought it over to Sarah.

"I want you to have this," he said.

The knife was as bright as polished silver.

"Thanks anyway," Sarah said, "but keep your knife."

"I want you to have it."

"Go ahead and take it," Dianne urged. "He has another one at home."

"It's an initiation gift," Mike told her.

Sarah hesitated, then finally took the knife.

"I guess I can wear it on the subway," she said.

Everyone wished everyone else goodnight; then Sarah and Phil walked off toward their tent.

They were inside getting undressed when Sarah remembered that she had to change her tampon again.

"I'll be back in a minute," she told Phil.

"Where are you going?"

"I'm still having my period."

She left the tent to take care of business, and when she came back, Phil was already snoring.

Day Three

Even though Sarah was tired, she had trouble falling asleep. It was the first time she had spent the night in a tent, and every strange noise was amplified.

There was a large insect in the tent that kept threatening to land on her face, and when it finally touched down on Sarah's nose, she poked her eye trying to swat it.

There were strange noises outside, too. Something was clawing at the side of the tent, and there was an animal off in the woods that made a noise like a chainsaw.

Although Sarah was lying on an ensolite pad and thought she had cleared the ground under the tent of all rocks and twigs, she still felt as if she were sleeping on a chain link fence. She tossed and turned and curled up in every possible shape, but there was no way to avoid the lumps.

"Are you still awake?" Phil asked her.

"I'm afraid so."

Phil turned on his side and leaned on his elbow.

"You're scared, aren't you? I used to be scared when I was a boy and went camping."

"I've always been a light sleeper. All these noises don't help."

"What about the sirens every night at home?"

"Those are familiar noises."

"You'll sleep better tomorrow. The first night is always the worst." Phil lay back down.

Sarah stared up at the tent a few moments, then said, "Do you ever feel like you're living in a dream?"

"Go to sleep."

"I was just lying here thinking how strange it is that we're all going to die someday."

"I don't usually have profound thoughts in the middle of the night."

"Don't make fun of it," Sarah said.

"You're having a religious experience. Believe me, it'll go away."

Sarah moved next to Phil and closed her eyes. A moment later she heard something walking not far from the tent.

"What was that?" she said.

"What was what?"

"That noise. I heard something outside."

"Go to sleep."

"I'm telling you that I heard something."

"Go to sleep."

Phil turned his back to Sarah and pulled the sleeping bag over his head. Sarah lay quiet, staring at the top of the tent, her ears perked for any sound.

Outside, something began to breathe—low and heavy.

"Quit fooling around," Phil said.

"That wasn't me."

Phil quickly rolled over and looked at her.

"Are you sure?" he said.

"I told you before that I heard something out there."

"Be quiet!"

They listened to the forest, but the only sound was the soft gurgle of the creek.

"Give me the flashlight," Phil said.

"Why?"

"I'm going to take a look."

"Don't you dare open those flaps."

"Give me the flashlight."

Sarah fumbled around in the back of the tent until she found the flashlight in one of Phil's boots and handed it to Phil. He unzipped the flaps just a few inches and directed the light outside.

"What do you see?" Sarah asked.

"Nothing. I have to open it up more."

"Are you crazy? It might come in here!"

Phil put down the flashlight and used both hands to open the zipper. When he was finished, he threw back the flap onto the tent.

Standing right in front of them was Mike Stove.

"You scared the hell out of me," Sarah said.

She picked up the flashlight and directed it upward, giving Mike's face an eerie starkness.

He crouched down and looked inside the tent.

"I think there was a bear prowling around," he said.

"A bear?" Sarah said.

"You don't have any food in here, do you?"

"I strung it up in the trees like you told us to," Phil said.

"Good. If you don't have food in your tent, there shouldn't be any problem."

"You mean it might come back?" Sarah said.

"That depends on how hungry it is."

"But if there's no food in here, it won't come inside, right?"

"There's only one other reason it might, but the bear would have to be starving."

"What's the reason?"

"It's only folklore, but some people swear it's true."

"What's true?"

Mike looked straight into Sarah's eyes and said, "A starving bear will sometimes attack a woman when she's having her period."

Sarah and Phil turned toward each other, their eyes wide. There was no need to say anything.

"I'll look around a little longer," Mike said. "You get a good night's sleep. We have a long day's hike tomorrow."

They said goodnight; then as soon as Mike left, Phil zipped up the flaps.

"Close them all the way," Sarah said.

"But we won't get any fresh air."

"Who cares? Close them."

When they were completely sealed up, Sarah noticed that Phil moved his sleeping bag farther to his side of the tent.

"Maybe I should sleep outside," Sarah said. "I don't want you attacked because of me."

"Don't be silly. You heard Mike. He said it was folklore."

"Right," Sarah said. "There's no truth to folklore, is there?"

A few minutes later, she could hear Phil snoring, and it made her jealous. Sarah imagined that each noise outside was the bear coming to get her.

Life was so unfair. Why didn't the men have to worry about being eaten by bears? Sarah was convinced that only the male bears would attack a woman because of her period. The females would be more understanding.

Maybe Bob Harwood was right—the back country was

no place for a woman. Not this woman anyway, Sarah thought.

For the next hour, Sarah pictured a giant bear standing on his hind legs, sniffing the air for the scent of her blood. She could see the saliva drooling from his mouth.

Meat, she thought. I'm nothing but a piece of meat.

Exhaustion finally overcame Sarah's fears, and she fell into a troubled sleep that lasted until the dull light of morning filled the tent.

When she woke, Sarah couldn't figure out where she was for a few moments. She felt stiff from head to toe.

Phil was asleep with his arm thrown across Sarah's chest. The more she thought about the weight of the arm, the heavier it felt, until she finally thought she was going to suffocate.

Panicky, she threw the arm off.

For half an hour, the campsite was quiet except for the morning chatter of birds and the icy sound of the creek.

Later, Rachel and Jim began to argue inside their tent. Their voices were muffled at first, but they became louder as the argument heated up.

"You drink too goddamn much," Rachel said.

"It's none of your business."

"You drink until your dick gets soggy, and we can't even screw."

"I'm sure you do fine by yourself."

"I don't need to do it myself. There are plenty of men willing to do it for me."

"I don't want to hear about it."

As Sarah continued to listen to the Wheatleys, she wondered how two people who hated each other so much could sleep in the same tent, much less live together every day. Their mutual cruelty far surpassed anything that Sarah had experienced in her marriage to Gary.

The marital bout continued for several more rounds before Mike Stove yelled for the Wheatleys to shut up. At last, quiet returned to the campsite.

At six-thirty Mike roused the hikers and told them to be ready to go in half an hour.

Sarah woke up Phil, and they got out of their sleeping bags and dressed into their wool clothes. As Sarah laced her boots, she noticed Phil examining his feet.

"Is anything wrong?" she asked.

"No."

"You better get some moleskin from Mike," Sarah said. "You're starting to get blisters."

Phil put on his socks.

"My feet will be fine, thank you."

"Why are you being so stubborn?"

"Just worry about your own feet, okay?"

"Excuse me for being concerned."

In a huff, Sarah threw on Mike's parka and left the tent.

Outside the ground was dry and the sky overcast. It felt much colder than the day before. Mike Stove already had a large fire going and was gathering wood in the nearby forest.

Sarah was shocked to see Jim and Rachel Wheatley cuddled together like two love birds in front of the fire.

"Let me get you some coffee," Rachel said to her cheerily.

She pooched out her lips and gave Jim a kiss, then got up to reach for the black enamel pot.

Sarah sat down next to Jim and searched for the hidden shame in his expression, but what she found looked more like love's afterglow.

Phil and Dianne came out of their tents a few minutes later, and as everyone huddled by the fire drinking coffee, Mike stood in front of them and began to speak in a noticeably serious tone of voice.

"I don't like the change in weather," he said. "I think it's going to snow."

"Are you sure?" Jim asked.

Mike pointed toward the sky.

"Those are cirrostratus clouds," he said. "They usually mean that a storm is about a day off. With this cold, I'd say that it's going to snow pretty hard."

"Since when are you afraid of the snow?" Phil asked.

"I'm not afraid of it. But we don't have the right gear. We should have gaiters for our boots, steeper walls on our tents, even snow shoes if it gets deep enough."

"I'm sure we can get by without the luxuries," Phil said.

"That's not all," Mike said. "It's easier to get wet, and that means it's easier to get hypothermia."

"What do you think we should do?" Sarah asked.

"If it was just me, I'd go on. I have experience with these things. For your sake, it might be easier to go back to the lodge."

"After coming this far?" Phil said.

"I thought you'd be glad to go back," Mike said with a smile.

"If you can go on, then I sure as hell can."

"How dangerous will it be if we continue?" Sarah asked.

"If you do what I tell you to do, it won't be dangerous, but there can't be any horsing around. It's time to start taking this hike seriously."

"If it isn't dangerous," Phil said, "then let's go on."

"I've got an idea," Rachel said. "Why don't you two guys go ahead, and the rest of us will go back to the lodge."

"You'd be lost in half an hour," Mike said.

"Dianne can lead us back."

"I don't know how to read a trail map," Dianne said.

"How hard can it be?"

Rachel walked up to Mike and asked for the map. She looked at it, puzzled a moment, then showed the map to Sarah. It was nothing but a hopeless maze of wavy lines and benchmarks.

"I can't read it either," Sarah said. "Maybe Mike can teach us."

"It would take too long," Mike said. "And besides, I need the map myself."

"This is ridiculous," Jim said. "I don't care whether we go on or return, but I think we ought to do it together."

"Jim's right," Dianne said.

Mike took back the map, folded it, and put it in his shirt pocket.

"It's up to you," he said. "But it'll get rougher if it snows."

"Rough is what we came here for," Phil said.

"Maybe you did," Rachel said, "but not me."

Phil cast her an ugly glance.

"I think we should go on," Jim said.

"Since when did you become so adventurous?" Rachel asked.

"We've come this far. We might as well finish."

Rachel turned to Sarah and Dianne.

"What do you want to do?" she asked.

"I'd rather go back," Sarah said.

"If we poop on the boys' parade, we'll never hear the end of it."

"I'm afraid you're right."

"What about you, Dianne?"

"I've never hiked in the snow. It might be fun."

"Then it's settled," Phil said happily. "Most of us want to go on and finish."

He looked around at the group. Sarah and Rachel appeared displeased, but didn't object.

"Let's eat breakfast and break camp," Mike said.

He walked off into the woods to untie his backpack, and slowly the group disbanded and followed him. One by one they returned to the campfire to make breakfast.

Sarah lit up her stove and boiled water for oatmeal while Phil rolled up their tent and sleeping bags. When he was finished, he went over near the fire next to Sarah, and she handed him a bowl of steaming oatmeal.

"It tastes a little pasty," he said.

"Then you can make it yourself next time."

"What are you so grumpy about?"

"I don't like being yelled at when I wake up."

"I didn't yell at you."

Phil looked over to make sure Mike wasn't listening.

"Look, I'm sorry about that," he said. "But it's damn important for me to finish this hike, and if Mike sees my feet, he'll make us go back."

"That's no excuse to ruin my trip. Remember, I didn't want to come in the first place."

"I'm sorry. What else can I say?"

"I'll try to think of something."

While the hikers were eating, Dianne suddenly told them to be quiet, and when they looked up, they saw a deer standing in the nearby woods.

Sarah had never seen a deer—much less one so close—and she marveled at its delicate beauty and shiny, jet black eyes. The deer sniffed around the campsite a few minutes hoping to get some breakfast; then Rachel sneezed, and the animal took off, bounding through the forest.

"There are plenty of deer around," Mike said. "They feed in the morning and evening."

"Wasn't it beautiful?" Sarah said to Phil.

"It would make some beautiful steaks."

"You're disgusting."

"I was only kidding."

Sarah offered to give Mike his parka back, but he insisted that he didn't need it. He said that a couple of wool sweaters covered by his nylon shell would be as warm as any parka.

After breakfast, when everyone was packed, the fire was buried, and the area was policed for trash, the hikers followed Mike back to the trail. With the overcast sky, the forest seemed gray and gloomy.

Sarah volunteered to carry Dianne's pack for the first two hours, and the two women walked together in the rear of the column.

Sarah felt stiff from the previous day's hike and from sleeping on the hard ground, but she was surprised to find that her leg muscles loosened up after a while, and she was fairly comfortable hiking.

Maybe Mike was right—jogging was starting to pay off after all.

Despite the nippy weather, Sarah was soon forced to strip off her jacket and sweater and walk in her wool shirt alone. Grinding her way up the slow-rising hills turned her body into a furnace, and she was amazed how much heat a bowl of oatmeal could generate.

"I noticed you haven't had a cigarette this morning," Dianne said.

"They taste funny out here."

"It's good you stopped. You won't get out of breath as easily."

"I'll probably start again when I get back home. It's hard to break old habits."

Dianne didn't know how to read trail maps, but Sarah learned that Dianne knew a lot about the plant life in the area. With a little instruction, Sarah was soon able to distinguish between the red pines with their two-needle clusters and the giant white pines with their clusters of five. She could spot a hemlock instantly by its small, pendant-shaped cone, and, although the forest was mostly coniferous, she learned to recognize the bark textures of the sugar maple and yellow birch. She learned that some plants—like the beautiful asters—not only survived the fall weather, but flowered in it.

Sarah was already beginning to adapt to the rugged terrain. Yesterday, when she placed her fingertips to her throat, she felt her heart racing, but this morning her pulse was slower and more regular, and her breathing was less hurried, too.

As she talked with Dianne, she learned to admire and perhaps be a little jealous of her. Dianne was living the life that Sarah was supposed to be living.

"I love my real estate work," Dianne said, "but I swear I couldn't stay away from the children as much as Mike does. I like watching them grow too much.

"At first I jumped at every promotion and business trip that came along, but then I saw what I was giving up."

Sarah thought that Dianne was a lot like Rachel in one regard—neither woman tried to change her husband. Instead, they charted his strong points and weak points and stayed clear of the shoals.

"How do you like insurance work?" Dianne asked.

"It's a paycheck."

"Have you looked around for anything else?"

"There's really nothing else to do. After Gary and I got married, I pulled out of college to support him. Then, after we separated, I needed the money too much to go back to school."

"What about night school?"

"I'm too tired when I get home."

"I know what you mean."

"Maybe this trip will give me more stamina," Sarah said. "It would be nice to come home after work and feel like doing something besides watching TV."

Just before the planned noon break, Sarah heard the distant sound of water grow louder as the group approached its source. She could smell the water's freshness even from far away. It was as if her senses were being keyed up by all the new sights and sounds and smells around her.

"We have to cross a river up ahead," Dianne said.

"That's the same one we'll run into again on the return trip, isn't it?"

"You have a good memory."

"Sometimes it's too good."

As the group hiked down through a ravine, the river suddenly came into view. It was a clear, hard-rushing river about two hundred feet wide with narrow bands of rapids crossing it in two places.

As Sarah made her way carefully down the hillside, her boots slipped in the loose soil, and she began to feel her heart rate quicken with anticipation.

She wondered if it wouldn't be a good idea to let Dianne

carry her own backpack across the river. It was stupid to tempt fate, and it was stupid not to admit to the others that she was scared. She had a right to be scared, she thought. She had almost drowned the day before.

"I thought the river would be smaller," she said to Dianne.

"Really, you don't have to worry. Just do whatever Mike says to do."

The water was rushing too swiftly to freeze, but Sarah could tell that it was cold as ice. It looked like water that wanted to be ice, and would have been ice, if the current had only let it.

The hikers stopped along the bank and surveyed the stretch of water.

"I'm going to find a place to cross," Mike said as he shed his backpack and laid it on the ground. "Wait here."

He took off his boots, rag socks, and liners, then rolled up his pants above the knees. His legs were muscular and tanned.

"Nice set of pegs," Rachel said. Then she turned to Jim. "You'd better keep your pants rolled down."

Sarah and the others watched Mike hike down along the bank until he reached a point slightly above-river from the narrow band of rapids. He stepped into the water and began to move slowly across, using his walking stick to feel out his way across the rock.

When he finally reached the other side, he turned back to the other hikers and waved his stick. Then he made the return trip in half the time.

"It's not bad," he announced when he got back.

"Your feet are red," Rachel said.

"The water's cold, but there's a nice ledge that runs straight across to the other side."

"It looks deep where we are," Sarah said.

"There are deep pools if you fall off the ledge," Mike said. "You'll have to be careful . . . especially you, Sarah."

Following Mike's example, the hikers took off their boots and tied them to their backpacks; then they rolled up their pants.

"You're not going to cross with that backpack, are you?" Phil said to Sarah.

If anyone else but Phil had asked the question, she would have said no.

"Of course I am."

Mike stepped forward.

"Give Dianne her backpack," he ordered Sarah. "I'm not going to fish you out of the water twice on this trip."

Sarah felt like kicking him in the ass.

"It's all right," Dianne said. "I'll take my pack across; then you can carry it all afternoon if you want to."

Sarah saw the hopelessness of her position. Even Rachel was looking at her as if she were being needlessly stubborn.

Reluctantly she took off the pack and gave it to Dianne.

When everyone was ready, Mike led them to the shallowest spot, where the hikers waded out into the icy water single file.

"Wow, that's cold!" Rachel shrieked.

Sarah's feet cramped up the moment they touched the water. She walked close behind Rachel, trying to memorize each step that Rachel took. The rock ledge they traveled on was deceptive—it looked flat, but sometimes it dipped down sharply, and the water came above the knees.

Throughout, Sarah kept a leery eye on the jagged stones and white-water rapids directly downstream.

"It's slick in through here," Mike shouted. "Be extra careful!"

The strength of the current pushed against Sarah's legs, sending water flaring off to both sides. It was like the water was trying to gently shove her over into the rapids.

Suddenly, Jim slipped and fell, opening a deep gash in his knee.

His pants were rolled up, and Sarah could see the bright blood carried away by the river.

Mike came over quickly to examine the injury.

"You'll be okay," he said. "A little BFI powder and a dressing, and you'll be ready to go."

"To tell you the truth, I feel a bit woozy," Jim said.

"Phil will take you the rest of the way," Mike said. "I want to get the girls across; then I'll fix you right up."

Phil came over and told Jim to lean on him; then they moved slowly toward the bank while Mike helped the women over a tricky section of the passage where the rock ledge turned into a series of submerged boulders.

When they were almost across, Mike took a position at the rear, just behind Sarah.

She could feel him breathing down her neck. It was hard enough to concentrate on not falling without the image of Mike looming behind her with his arms out, ready to grab her.

Why didn't he go bother Dianne or Rachel? she thought. Why didn't he get the hell away and stop making her feel so helpless?

Suddenly she heard Mike yell, and, turning around fast, she saw him being swept off the ledge into the white water.

Sarah was shocked and afraid at first, but Mike quickly sprang up in the chest-high water and signaled that he was all right.

Rachel laughed as she, Dianne, and Sarah raced over to help Mike get back onto the rock.

"Give me your hand!" he shouted angrily. "I'm freezing my balls off!"

"We don't want that to happen," Rachel said.

Mike unbuckled his belt and pack frame and handed them to Sarah. Water was pouring out of his pack and the barrel of his gun.

The first time that Mike tried to step onto the ledge, the slippery rock and hard-rushing water made him fall back again.

"Can't you pull any harder than that!" Mike screamed at the women.

"Don't be nasty," Rachel teased. "We don't have the upper body development that you do."

With Sarah and Dianne holding on to Rachel to brace her, Rachel leaned over and grabbed Mike's arm. This time, he was able to get one leg up on the ledge and pull himself to his knees with the women's help.

"You could have worked a little faster," Mike huffed.

He was standing there looking quite ridiculous, his hair flattened, his clothes soaked, his face scarlet with a mixture of embarrassment and anger. Simultaneously, the women broke out laughing at him.

"You have a sick idea of what's funny," Mike said.

He grabbed his gear and took off for the bank.

"He might be a little hard to live with for a while," Dianne said.

"I'd swear off sex for a month if I could have a picture of him standing in the water," Rachel said.

"Let's go," Sarah said. "I can't even feel my toes anymore."

The women waded to the bank and helped each other climb up. Then they put on their socks and boots and walked back into the woods, where the men were assembled.

"It's a mite cold to go swimming, isn't it?" Phil teased.

Mike ignored the remark and looked at Jim's knee.

"That cut will have to wait until I change my clothes," he said.

"I can take care of him," Sarah said.

"Sure."

"I'm serious. I took a first aid course."

Mike looked at her incredulously a moment, then said, "Okay. I'm going to change my clothes. You take care of Jim."

He paused a moment—almost as if he expected Sarah to confess that she didn't know a thing about first aid—then he gathered together some reasonably dry clothes and took off behind the trees.

"I didn't know you took a first aid course," Phil said.

"I could fill that river down there with all the things you don't know about me."

Sarah told Jim to sit on his backpack and bend his knee; then she covered the wound with antiseptic powder, dressed it with gauze, and began to wrap the wound with a bandage.

Phil looked on with great interest as Sarah first wrapped the bandage around the dressing, then wrapped one end around the upper leg and the other around the lower. Then she split the end of the bandage and tied it around Jim's leg with a knot.

"That should do it," she told Jim.

Mike Stove returned in a dry set of clothes and inspected Sarah's job.

"Nice work," he said. "I'm impressed."

Phil and Mike helped Jim stand up, and everyone watched as he took his first provisional steps. Soon he was walking without a limp.

"Good as new," Jim said.

He thanked Sarah and told her to send the bill to Mike.

"I'm going to sue him for criminal neglect," Jim said, "just as soon as we get back to New York."

"If you're not more careful, you might not get back to New York," Mike said.

Dianne and Rachel scoured the nearby woods for firewood, while the others prepared to eat lunch. Sarah boiled water to reconstitute some macaroni and cheese, but when it was ready, Phil was gone.

Sarah told the others that she would be back in a minute; then she went off to find out what had happened to Phil.

She eventually found him down by the river. He was bathing his feet in the cold water. He turned around startled when Sarah said, "Your blisters have gotten worse, haven't they?"

Phil looked away.

"I thought my feet would get better if I took it easier," he said.

"Let me have a look," Sarah said.

When Phil withdrew his feet from the water, Sarah was shocked by the size of the blisters. The cellophane-like skin was puffed up as large as silver dollars in some places, and a couple of the blisters were popped and rubbed raw.

"Don't ever tell me I'm stubborn again," Sarah said. "I'm going to get Mike."

"Give me a break, Sarah. You can handle this. Why does Mike have to know?"

"He has more experience with these things."

"He'll only make us go back," Phil said.

"Maybe that's the best thing."

Phil shook his head in frustration.

When Sarah returned with Mike, she carried a small first aid kit. Mike got down on one knee, checked Phil's blisters, and said, "You horse's behind. Why didn't you tell me about this earlier?"

Sarah was about to explain why, but then decided that Phil's ego was taking enough of a bruising already.

"Do you think they're infected?" she asked Mike.

"I don't like all the redness."

"It looks puffy between the toes."

"Maybe a little."

Mike looked the blisters over again; then he stood up.

"Let's carry him back to the fire," he said.

"I can walk by myself," Phil said.

"You stay put. You've caused enough trouble already, and I don't want you to get your feet dirty."

Phil started arguing, but Sarah told him to shut up.

While Phil held on to his socks and boots, Sarah bent

down and picked up his legs, and Mike lifted him under his arms.

"Can you handle him?" Mike asked.

"Sure," Sarah said. "You've got the heavy end."

"I feel stupid," Phil said.

With Sarah leading the way, they brought Phil up the side of the bank into the trees and carried him back to the campfire.

"What happened?" Dianne asked as Mike and Sarah rested Phil on a poncho.

"It's not serious," Sarah said. "He's got some blisters."

Sarah told Mike that she would take care of Phil. The other hikers gathered around to watch.

Explaining each step of the procedure, Sarah cleaned the opened blisters and dressed them. Then she heated the end of Mike's pocket knife in the fire.

"What are you going to do with that?" Phil asked.

"We'll drain the blisters that haven't popped yet, so they don't tear. There's less chance they'll get infected."

Carefully, with Phil and the others grimacing with the anticipation of pain, Sarah cut tiny slits in the remaining blisters and squeezed out the clear fluid underneath. Then she dressed the blisters and applied moleskin patches to other areas of the feet that looked tender.

"That didn't hurt at all," Phil said with obvious relief. "Thanks, Sarah."

Mike told him to change his socks every couple of hours and wash out the old ones.

"Hang them on your pack, and they'll dry out. If you need more, Jim and I will lend you some."

"Do we have to go back to the lodge?" Phil asked him.

"It's two days back and three days forward. As long as you can walk, I don't see any reason to get you back one day earlier."

"Good."

"We'll have to slow down the pace though."

"That will be better for me, too," Jim said.

Phil stood up and walked around.

"They feel great," Phil said. "I'll be able to make it."

"Don't push it though," Mike said. "And take good care of yourself, or I'll have to carry you back myself."

"Not a chance," Phil said.

When the fire was out, and the hikers were once again top-heavy with their packs, they followed Mike to the trail and began the afternoon journey to Sturgeon Lake, where Mike said they would camp for the night.

It still hadn't snowed, but Mike pointed out the dull halo around the sun and said it was another sure sign.

Sarah walked alongside Phil for the first hour to see how he held up; then she noticed that Jim was all alone in the rear, having fallen back a few hundred feet from the others.

Sarah told Phil she'd be back in a few minutes; then she waited alongside the trail until Jim caught up to her.

"Is it the leg?" she asked.

"No, it's fine. I wanted to be alone for a while."

"Okay," Sarah said, and she started to walk back to the others.

"Wait a minute," Jim said. "Let's talk."

"Sure, if you want to."

Jim came up alongside her, and they walked abreast through the gray forest, their breath steamy as they labored up the hill.

"I couldn't help hearing the fight you had with Rachel this morning," Sarah said.

"We fight every morning. It's habitual, like the first cup of coffee. Nothing special."

"Phil told me that you wrote for a newspaper at one time."

"That's right . . . in Cleveland."

"How'd you end up writing insurance policies?"

"You might say that my job began to interfere with my drinking."

Jim laughed, but it sounded like it hurt.

"When did you meet Rachel?" Sarah asked.

"The first day I came to New York, Rachel rear-ended my car."

"You're kidding."

"As a matter of fact, she's been rear-ending me ever since."

"You're exaggerating."

"Not at all. It's no secret that our marriage stinks."

"If it's so bad, why don't you get out of it?"

"I can't."

"You can always get out of it. It hurts like hell sometimes, but you can do it."

70

"This is different. Rachel threatened to kill herself if I ever leave her."

"That doesn't sound like Rachel at all."

"Most people don't know her. She's more fragile than you think . . . crueler, too."

"I wouldn't call her cruel."

"She's a dream killer. Anytime I wanted to do something special with my life, Rachel got jealous and ruined my chances. I was working on a novel for six years, and, just when I was getting ready to send it out, Rachel burned it with all my notes."

"Why would she do that?"

"I'm going to tell you a story about Rachel, but you have to promise never to tell anyone else. And you can't let Rachel know that I told you."

"I don't think I want to get involved in that kind of thing," Sarah said.

"You have to hear it. You can't understand Rachel until you do."

Sarah was reluctant to get so involved in the Wheatleys' stormy lives, but she didn't see how she could avoid it without hurting Jim.

"Okay," she said.

Jim began to tell Sarah about Rachel's childhood—the death of her mother at an early age and the years she spent with her drunken, usually unemployed father.

"It's incredible she even survived," Jim said with what Sarah sensed was a tone of admiration. "Rachel lived in an unheated house most of the time because her father couldn't afford the oil or wasn't around. She went to school one day with a bad cold, and, when her teacher questioned her, she discovered that Rachel was sleeping with her father to stay warm, and her father was sexually abusing her."

"I've heard about that happening, but I still can't imagine it," Sarah said.

"Rachel didn't understand it at the time, but later she became very bitter."

"What did they do to her father?"

"The courts removed Rachel to a foster home, and she spent the rest of her childhood moving from place to place. Her father was hospitalized not long after and died of cirrhosis."

71

"What a lousy way to have to grow up."

"She needs me a lot more than she lets on," Jim said.

Sarah reached over and gave Jim's hand a gentle squeeze.

"I'm sorry to dump all this on you," he said.

"Not at all. I'm glad you did."

As they continued to walk through the morning chill, Sarah thought to herself how small her own problems were in comparison to Jim's. His pain and her memory of pain bonded them closely together.

Phil seemed much improved as time went on, but the group stuck to a slower pace, and Mike sometimes checked Phil's blisters. Phil eventually admitted that he hadn't softened his boots the way Mike had directed the hikers to do before they left New York.

"I didn't have time," Phil said. "Besides, when you shell out eighty dollars for boots, the least they can do is not tear your feet to shreds."

During the three o'clock break, Sarah was sitting alone on a fallen tree, looking into the deep woods, when Phil came up to her with a handful of wild flowers.

"I want to call a truce between us," he said.

Sarah moved over and let Phil sit beside her. She took the flowers and smelled their fragrance. She wondered how anything so delicate and beautiful could survive in this land.

"Why a truce?" she said. "We haven't fought for almost nine hours."

"We fight too often. I don't like it."

"Then all we have to do is promise never to fight again."

"Okay, let's promise."

They sealed the pact with a kiss.

"How do you feel about the hike so far?" Phil asked.

"Let's say that I'm adjusting."

"I'm proud of the way you're hanging in there . . . especially after the beating you took yesterday."

"That's nice of you to say. You can be pretty sweet when you want to be."

"You talk as if all we do is fight."

"I'm only kidding."

"No, you're not. You always make our relationship look worse than it is."

72

"Let's just say I'm skeptical about relationships."

"I'm trying hard to understand what your marriage did to you, Sarah, but I swear I can't. So you made a mistake. So what? Lots of people do, but that doesn't stop them from falling in love with someone else."

"That's easy for you to say. You didn't get creamed like I did."

Mike Stove interrupted by calling for everyone to get ready to move out. Phil got up and helped Sarah on with her backpack; then she returned the favor.

As they started out after Mike, Phil turned to Sarah and said, "If you really love someone strongly enough, you're willing to take risks."

"Maybe that's our problem," she said. "I'm not willing."

Phil didn't respond, but he looked hurt, and Sarah wished she hadn't opened her big mouth.

The first sight of Sturgeon Lake came as the hikers reached the summit of a ridge and looked down on the lake's immense frozen beauty. It seemed to flow around the hills, working its fingers gently into every fold.

The hikers made their way down a switchback trail, catching occasional glimpses of the lake through the white pines, until they broke out of the forest onto the rocky shoreline.

Mike Stove suddenly held up his arm and motioned for the group to stop. Not more than two hundred yards to the right, there was a large moose, iron-gray in color, nibbling on some vegetation in the lake.

"Look!" Sarah whispered excitedly to Phil. "It's a real goddamn moose!"

The hikers watched in silence as the animal continued to eat, until it sensed their presence and galloped out of sight into the forest.

"That was a big one," Mike said. "Those antlers must have been five feet wide."

Just as he finished speaking, there was a hollow, echoing boom that rolled through the forest—like the sound of an ax striking a tree.

"What the hell was that?" Rachel said.

"It's the moose," Mike said. "Sounds kind of eerie, doesn't it?"

There was something about seeing "a real goddamn

moose" that made Sarah realize the wilderness of the area they were in even more than anything else so far.

Mike led the hikers along the shoreline for close to twenty minutes before he finally stopped and said in an almost prophetic voice, "There's the spot."

He pointed his walking stick toward an open area in the forest, not thirty yards back, with a clear view of the lake.

With a habitualness that made Sarah think she had lived in the wilderness most of her life, she and the others went about their chores—clearing the ground, pitching the tents, gathering wood for the fire, lashing a biffy to the trees, and unpacking enough food for the evening meal.

"There's enough time to hike to some waterfalls before it gets dark," Mike said. "They're down there to the left about a mile."

"No way," Jim said. "I'm going to take a nap, then eat dinner."

"That's a good idea," Phil said as he carefully removed his boots. "My feet have seen enough walking for today."

Mike turned to Sarah.

"Not me," she said. "I could use a nap, too."

"Okay, but Harwood tells me it's really worth it."

Dianne and Rachel also declined the offer, Dianne saying that she, too, thought a short nap was the best idea.

Mike Stove looked on as Sarah showed Phil how to change his own dressings.

"My feet look better, don't they?" Phil asked Mike.

"The blisters have dried up some. But you're not out of the woods yet."

"I told you I'd be all right."

While Rachel continued to build up the fire, and Mike cut bigger logs with his bow saw, the other hikers unpacked their sleeping bags and went to their tents.

Sarah and Phil rolled out their pads and sleeping bags next to each other. Sarah felt proud of herself—she had kept up with the others today, and she was confident that she would be fine for the rest of the trip.

She and Phil undressed and crawled into their sleeping bags. Phil leaned over and kissed Sarah; then she closed her eyes and listened to the crackling fire until she dozed off.

When she woke up, Sarah looked at her watch and saw that she had slept about forty minutes. Phil was still sleeping.

Sarah quietly dressed and put on Mike's parka before slipping out of the tent.

The evening air was still. The campsite was deserted. Sarah enjoyed the peaceful atmosphere as she walked to the lake shore and stared out across the wide expanse of ice that stretched all the way to the treeline on the opposite shore.

She could smell the heavy scent of pine.

The beauty and serenity of the moment lulled Sarah into a dreamy mood until she noticed that the fire was almost out, and she went to gather wood. When she returned to the fire, she threw on some smaller branches, then placed some logs on top. The fire began to billow up with white smoke until the branches finally burst into flame. Sarah threw on two more logs for good measure; then, feeling that the fire would burn for some time without attendance, she walked back over to the side of the lake.

Sarah felt strangely at home in the forest, even after so short a time. It was as if part of her had been there all the time.

Maybe this was the "high" the Stoves talked about.

As she strolled to the left along the shoreline, Sarah watched two birds chase each other in large circles above the lake. Just a few days ago, she could have cared less what kind of birds they were, but now she wanted to know the names of everything.

Close to her feet the water lapped on the pebbly shore. The lake was free of ice for maybe fifty feet out, but from that point on it was frozen as far as she could see.

How boring it would be to go back to New York, she thought. It was too bad she couldn't package just a few pine trees, a hill or two, and maybe a jar of fresh air to open up on a lousy day at work.

The very idea of going back to work was depressing. How many more years would she endure the same dead-end job?

It felt grand to be walking here, bundled up in a warm parka with the cold nipping at her cheeks. It felt grand to be walking alone.

As she continued to walk, Sarah toyed with the idea of hiking to the falls.

Mike had said that they were a mile away, so it wouldn't take any longer than an hour to get there and back. And there was at least that much daylight remaining.

How could she get lost if she followed the lake all the way?

Sarah felt excited as she picked up the pace and started on her adventure. Out of sight of the campsite, she was struck in an immediate way by how small she was in comparison to everything around her. On the left, the giant pines towered overhead. On her right, lay the vast frozen lake. The narrow shore where she was walking was like a thin line dividing the two worlds.

Sarah stopped fast when she saw something brown and furry quite a distance ahead, by the edge of the lake. She couldn't tell what the animal was, but she was cautious because of her ignorance about wildlife in the back country. She had no idea which animals could hurt her and which ones couldn't.

Sarah walked forward slowly until she realized that the animal was a beaver. She recognized the dark, pancake tail. Before she could get any closer though, the animal ran back into the forest.

The excitement of catching a beaver out in the open soon melted when Sarah realized that she could just as easily have stumbled onto a bear. As she continued to hike, she kept one eye glued to the dark treeline.

For a second she wished that Phil were with her, but then she thought how foolish that was—Phil didn't know any more than she did. She was just as safe without him.

Suddenly a large bird exploded into flight right behind her, and Sarah screamed as she spun around in time to see the bird soar off across the lake.

When Sarah reached the twenty-minute mark and still couldn't hear the falls, she began to wonder if it wouldn't be best to turn around and go back to camp. It seemed to be getting darker more quickly than she had expected, and, though she remained confident that she couldn't possibly become lost, she didn't like the idea of walking in the forest after dusk.

Rather than go back, she decided to walk to the point of land up ahead, a journey she calculated would take no more than five or ten minutes; then she would turn around and go back.

As it turned out, the decision to delay her return was a good one because, when she reached the point, she saw where the water from the lake funneled off into a stream that headed out of sight into the forest. In the not too far distance, she could hear the rumbling of the falls.

Sarah followed a deer trail alongside the stream until she could see mist rising into the air and the sound became all-enveloping. The deer trail took a sudden sharp drop that she guessed would lead to the base of the falls, but she couldn't actually see the falls yet because of a wall of boulders in the way.

The mist continued to rise all around her as she carefully descended the steep trail. She was concentrating so entirely on not losing her footing that, when she finally looked up, she was amazed to see that the entire forest around her was glazed with ice—a regular crystal palace formed by the freezing mist.

She felt as if she had entered some kind of fantasy land, as far removed from the common earth as anything she had ever seen.

To get a view of the falls, Sarah squeezed through a narrow passage in the boulders, and she came out on a rock slab directly next to the thundering water. She looked up to where the stream leapt off the cliff and fell down the dizzying heights into a clear basin below.

Sarah was mesmerized by the spectacle and fury. The falls seemed to lift her spirits, quicken her pulse. The water was fresh and alive, filled with vital energy.

As she continued to gaze at the falls, she heard a loud, high-pitched cry, like the cry of an animal. She tried to peer over the edge of the slab down below, but she couldn't see anything but the basin and a lot of dense underbrush.

The cry sounded again, and Sarah thought this time that it seemed almost human. She quickly squeezed back through the boulders to the deer trail and practically slid on her bottom the rest of the way to the base of the falls. She crawled through the dense underbrush that shattered like delicate glass as she broke the ice glazing.

When the basin finally came into view, Sarah was shocked to see Mike Stove and Rachel Wheatley standing in the shelter of some boulders with their pants down to their ankles. Sarah slunk back into cover and watched dumbfounded as the pair continued to make love. Mike was driving Rachel up against a rock while she arched her neck and cried aloud.

Suddenly Mike exploded like the water dashing onto the

77

rocks, and Rachel squeezed her thighs around his hips in a frenzied, grunting climax.

When it was over, Rachel slid down the side of the rock, and the couple hurriedly dressed.

Sarah slipped away and ran back through the bushes to the deer trail. Out of breath, she scrambled up the steep trail until she reached the level of the stream; then she ran back alongside the lake as fast as she could to make certain that Mike and Rachel wouldn't see her.

As darkness took over the forest, Sarah dashed back to the campsite, wondering what to do. It was important not to get caught in a contradiction about where she had been, and it was hard to think straight when she was running hard and out of breath and feeling stupid and embarrassed and confused and angry, and how was she ever going to look Mike or Rachel in the face without remembering what she had seen?

Before she reached camp, Sarah was met by Jim and Phil.

"Where the hell were you?" Phil yelled. "We've been looking everywhere. You scared us out of our minds!"

"Take it easy," Jim said.

"Stay out of this, Wheatley."

Sarah explained that she had simply gone for a walk along the lake. "I didn't know I was required to clear all my activities with you in advance," she said.

"You could have left a goddamn note," Phil continued to rant. "Don't you have a fucking brain in your head?"

"I don't want to discuss it anymore," Sarah said, and she turned away from Phil and started back to camp.

Phil continued to nip at her heels, but Sarah wasn't paying any attention. Her mind was preoccupied, wondering how she would face Dianne.

Not far from the clearing, Dianne was waiting for them.

"You had us a little worried," she said.

"I went for a walk," Sarah said. "Believe me, I wouldn't have gone if I had known it was going to cause all this trouble."

"Did you run into Mike and Rachel?"

"No."

"They went to the falls while the rest of us were napping."

"They must have left before I did," Sarah said.

Sarah and Dianne walked together through the trees into the light of the campsite. After they sat down, Phil stormed over.

"Don't you realize how goddamn stupid it was for you to walk off at night?" he said.

"Leave her alone," Jim said quietly. "You've made your point."

Phil walked quickly up in front of him.

"You're really getting on my nerves, Wheatley."

"I don't understand why you're so pissed off. Look at yourself—you're acting like an idiot."

Without warning, Phil knocked Jim to the ground with the back of his fist.

Jim looked more startled than hurt as Sarah and Dianne ran over and helped him back onto his feet.

"I'm all right," Jim said.

As if the violent eruption had spent Phil's anger, he walked off to his tent and disappeared inside.

"That bastard," Sarah said.

"I shouldn't have said anything to him. He was worried about you."

"I swear I've never seen him act like that before," Sarah said.

There was a rustling of branches, and Mike and Rachel stepped out of the darkness into the firelight.

Their cheeks were still ruddy.

"It was a total waste of time," Rachel said as she sat down near the fire. "I've never been so disappointed in my life."

Mike kissed Dianne on the cheek, then noticed Jim rubbing his jaw.

"What happened to you?" he asked.

With great embarrassment, Sarah filled in the details.

"I don't blame Phil a bit," Mike said gruffly. "It was stupid for you to go off on your own."

Sarah had to bite her tongue.

"You didn't go to the falls, did you?" Rachel asked.

"No," Sarah said, "but from what you say, I didn't miss a thing."

"It was a real bore."

With total darkness now surrounding the campsite, the hikers prepared their dinner around the campfire as a breeze started to blow in from the lake. Previous meals had been characterized by conversation and laughter, but this one passed in silence.

Still upset by Phil's outburst and what she had seen down at the falls, Sarah picked at her beef stew without any appetite.

A deep chill set its teeth into her back as she huddled next to Dianne for warmth.

"I don't think I can sleep with Phil tonight," she said.

"You can stay with me," Dianne said. "Mike enjoys sleeping under the stars."

"No way," Mike said. "I'm not taking sides in their fight."

"It's not taking sides," Dianne said. "You can do it for one night until they get things straightened out."

"I told you no."

Dianne got up from the log and took Mike over into the trees. She talked to him in a hushed voice, so that the others couldn't hear.

Sarah could see Mike's expression gradually softening. She stood up and scraped her food off the plate into the fire. The gooey sauce dripped down the side of a log and bubbled up into a cloud of steam.

Soon Dianne returned with the predictable answer.

"Mike says it's fine. He'll sleep outside tonight."

"Thanks," Sarah said. "I think I'll turn in now."

Just before she turned to leave, she saw Mike lean Dianne against a tree and kiss her a long time.

Sarah's mind flashed back to the falls, and she became even more depressed.

After wishing Jim and Rachel a half-hearted goodnight, Sarah went to her tent to get her own sleeping bag.

When she crawled inside, she could tell that Phil was pretending to be asleep.

"You phony," she said.

Phil opened his eyes, but, before he could say a word, Sarah yanked her pad and bag from the tent and walked away.

Inside the Stoves' tent, she felt around in the dark for Mike's sleeping bag; then she rolled it up loosely and set it outside in front of the tent.

She stripped down to her fishnet underwear and put on a fresh pair of socks because the others felt damp. Then she got inside her sleeping bag and waited for the chill to go away.

She could hear the others outside talking around the campfire. She couldn't make out any of the conversation, but it was often broken by Rachel's sharp-edged laughter.

Sarah hated Rachel and hated Mike, too. She hated them for making a sucker of Dianne, who was an unsuspecting person, the kind of person who was always going to be taken for a ride by people like Mike and Rachel . . . and Gary, too, for that matter.

They were nothing more than predatory shitbirds, gobbling up food without a thought about what they were doing and whom they were hurting. And the worst part was that the predatory shitbirds didn't look a bit different from all the other birds, so you could easily end up hanging around with one of them and even falling in love with one, and, in the end, being torn to shreds by one before you knew what the hell you were into.

The more Sarah looked at it, the more she became convinced that the best way to handle relationships between the sexes was to avoid them completely.

It was a grim thought—as grim as it was unrealistic—and, as Sarah lay on her back, she watched the walls of the tent billow up and sink with her feelings.

Day Four

The locomotive roar of the wind sounded like it started in the faraway hills and rumbled toward her louder and louder until it was directly upon her. Sarah could hear the trees creaking all around her as she curled up inside her sleeping bag, burying her head under the covers.

"Are you awake?" Dianne asked.

"Yes. What's going on out there?"

Suddenly there was a crack, like the sound of lightning exploding right outside the tent, and moments later a branch struck the ground with a heavy thud.

"Let's go!" Dianne shouted as she scrambled out of her sleeping bag.

They dressed as fast as they could while the violent winds pressed the walls of the tent against them.

Sarah put on her pants backwards in her haste, but there wasn't time to straighten them out. She crawled from the tent and stood up as a blast of cold air slammed against her. She pulled the cord on her hood closed and looked at the wildly bending trees and the flapping tents, which seemed as if they might rip apart at any moment.

Only thirty feet behind her tent, Sarah discovered the gigantic branch that had fallen just a few minutes ago. She knew that if it had struck the tent, she would have been crushed.

Mike Stove was already busy at work taking down his tent, looking more like he was wrestling with it, while Dianne woke up the other hikers.

When everyone was outside, Mike told them to get to the lakeshore right away.

Phil stopped to get his pack down from the trees.

"Did you hear me?" Mike screamed at him. "Get your ass over by the lake!"

With the wind continuing to batter the forest, the group

hurried to the water's edge and stood huddled together, their backs to the tempest, while Mike Stove brought his tent from the campsite.

"Help me put this up," he told Phil.

"What's happening?" Jim yelled.

"I'm not sure, but we have to get under cover."

The tent was hurriedly erected with everyone pitching in to hold it down against the gusting winds. Then all six hikers crowded inside, shoulder-to-shoulder.

Outside, the wind screamed through the forest, and branches were constantly splitting and crashing to the ground.

"It sounds like a hurricane," Rachel said.

"It's not a hurricane," Mike said, "but the winds are hurricane strength."

"How long will it last?" Jim asked.

"I don't know. There's some kind of front coming through."

"Is that good or bad?"

"That depends on what's on the other side."

Sarah was squeezed tightly between Jim and Rachel, and Dianne, Phil, and Mike were lined up on the other side. The tent caved in on the sides whenever it was hit by one of the strong gusts.

"What if we have to stay in here all day?" Rachel asked.

"Then we stay all day," Mike said.

"I have a pack of cards in my backpack," Rachel said. "We could play strip poker to pass the time."

Everyone laughed, except Sarah.

The hikers remained in the cramped tent for over an hour, listening to the forest rage outside. Sarah kept expecting hail or snow, but none came.

Mike opened the flaps to see what was happening, and Sarah noticed several deer run through the campsite, looking as frightened as she was.

Though the wind chill brought the temperature well below zero, Sarah felt warm enough inside the tent. The tight weave of the nylon effectively broke the wind's back, and with Mike's down parka and the heat coming from everyone's bodies, she felt warm and snug.

As soon as the storm slackened a little, Mike said it was time to go out. The hikers piled out of the tent, and when Sarah stood up she saw that the trees were still bending wildly.

The Wheatleys' self-supporting tent had broken free of its stakes and had tumbled twenty yards or so into some brambles. The nylon wall was ripped, but Mike said he could fix it with duct tape. The hikers quickly took down their tents and carried everything back to the lakeshore.

It was almost impossible to eat. Everything that wasn't nailed down blew away, and, eventually, most of the group settled for eating a few handfuls of gorp.

Sarah spent most of her time talking to Jim and completely ignored Phil.

When everyone had eaten and was packed to go, Mike led them around the lake for several miles until they went back into the forest. The trees continued to bend and sway, and Sarah would have preferred to stay by the lake until the wind died down much more. But Mike insisted that it was safe enough to continue.

"This is what I call real backpacking," Mike said. "Now we'll see who the cry babies are."

But Sarah thought that Mike was more worried than he let on. Perhaps he knew he had made a mistake in not turning back when the weather went sour yesterday, but he was too proud to admit it. If being a cry baby meant not taking foolish risks, then Sarah was willing to admit that she was one of them.

A dead tree crashed to the ground not thirty yards from the trail, taking two smaller pines with it, and Sarah looked over at Jim with great alarm.

Mike Stove plodded on without losing a step.

The entire forest had changed radically. Yesterday it was a static world with the sky and trees all fixed as if in a painting, but today everything was in violent motion—the dark clouds rolled overhead, the trees bent like grass in a meadow. There was no sign of wildlife.

The constant noise from the wind made it a labor to be heard. Unlike previous days, when there was much banter, this morning the hikers were each bundled up in the solitude of their parkas with their hoods pulled over their heads and the tie strings closed to protect their faces from the stinging wind.

During one of the breaks, Sarah suggested to Dianne that it would be better to stop and wait for the storm to blow over, but Dianne insisted that Mike knew what he was doing and that Sarah's fears were only a result of her inexperience in the back country.

"What happens if this turns into a blizzard?" Sarah asked.

"If it starts snowing with all this wind, I'm sure we'll hold up until it passes over," Dianne said. "Mike knows plenty of ways to stay warm in the worst kind of weather. You really shouldn't worry."

But Sarah did worry, and Jim was worrying, too.

"Do you really think he knows what he's doing?" Sarah asked him.

"He knows a lot, but he can be awfully pig-headed, too."

"He's like that in the office sometimes."

"I know what you mean. That's why he's one of the best agents. He drives himself like a mad man."

"That's fine as long as he doesn't drive us, too," Sarah said.

"I'll talk to him next time we stop for a break."

A couple of hours beyond the lake, the terrain grew more rugged. Jutting faces of rock projected from the ground everywhere, sometimes forming steep cliffs that rose hundreds of feet. Sarah noticed that the trees on top of the rock were clinging to a mere handful of soil at times, and she became even more afraid that the wind would tear them loose.

Even though Sarah wasn't carrying a pack, she frequently stumbled over the rocks. The last thing in the world she needed now was to twist her ankle and have to be carried.

Whenever a stiff gust hit Sarah directly in the face, the cold became unbearable. Even with her thermal underwear, layers of clothes, and parka, she could feel the heat being sapped from her body by the strong winds. She and the other hikers had wrapped scarves around their faces to protect their cheeks and noses from frostbite, but the icy wind made her eyes water and gave her a terrible headache.

After three hours, when they stopped for their usual break, Mike led the hikers into a cave, so they would be sheltered from the wind. Everyone took off their packs, drank from their canteens, and ate dried fruit or candy to keep up their energy and warmth.

Jim Wheatley went over to Mike, who was sitting on his pack studying his trail map in the light from the cave's entrance.

"Maybe we should stay here until the weather simmers down," Jim said.

Mike looked up with an expression of strained patience.

"Go have another drink, and let me worry about the weather," he said.

"There's no need for that. I was only making a simple suggestion."

"It was one I'd expect from a simpleton."

"I don't think it's smart to be walking around in the woods during a windstorm."

"Is that based on all your years of backpacking experience?"

"It's based on common sense. You don't need any experience to see trees falling on top of your head."

Mike finally put away his map and stood up.

Sarah was afraid something would happen, so she told Jim to forget it.

"No, no," Jim said. "We have a right to ask questions. It's our lives."

"I should have known better than to bring a drunk on a hiking trip," Mike said. "Especially one who's scared like an old woman."

"Is that what this is all about—proving how tough you are?"

"You're a drunk and a coward."

"And if you're risking our lives to prove that, then you're an even bigger jackass than I thought you were."

Mike grabbed Jim's throat and bounced his head against the rock. Sarah and Dianne ran over to pull Mike off.

"Let him go!" Dianne yelled as she tugged on his arm.

Rachel was laughing in the background.

"I want this ginhead to know that he can't get away talking shit to me out here. He can get away with it back in New York, but not out here!"

Jim was gagging by the time Mike finally set him back on his feet and released him.

Sarah was furious.

"You're a goddamn Neanderthal," she yelled.

Mike looked down at Sarah and broke into a thin smile, as though he thought Sarah's little outburst was cute.

"Didn't you hear me?" she yelled in his face. "I called you a name. Aren't you going to beat on me, too?"

"Come on," Dianne said, taking Sarah's arm gently. "Come over here with me."

"I want Mike to apologize right now."

"Come with me. Mike has enough worries already."

"I don't accept that," Sarah said. "And I'm sick of you defending him. They ought to give you a medal for it."

"That's not fair."

"Forget it," Jim told Sarah.

"No, I'm not going to forget it. Ever since we've come here, Mike's been acting like a gorilla."

"Sarah will feel better after she and Phil start screwing again," Mike said laughingly.

The sophomoric remark exploded like a bomb in Sarah's head. Before she could stop herself, the words came shooting back.

"Did you feel better after you screwed Rachel yesterday?" she said.

Mike turned red and instantly denied the accusation, but Sarah could tell that the damage was already done. The look on Dianne's face made it plain that she believed her.

"I'm sorry," Sarah said. "I didn't mean to hurt you."

Dianne walked out of the cave without saying a word.

"Nice work," Phil said to Sarah.

As Mike rushed past to follow his wife, he gave Sarah a look of utter contempt.

"I don't believe I did that," Sarah said.

"It's not your fault," Jim said. "The whole vacation was a bad idea to begin with. The sooner we get back to New York the better."

Mike was outside talking to Dianne for almost half an hour before he finally came back into the cave and told everyone to put on their packs. Sarah could hardly bear to look him in the face as he walked over to her and faced her square.

"I want you and Jim to know that I have never put this group in danger to prove anything to myself or to any one of you," he said.

With that, Mike picked up his and Dianne's backpacks and headed outside. In silence, the other hikers followed him.

The rest of the day into late afternoon, the wind continued without a break, and the dark clouds swept across the sky.

The predicted snow failed to appear.

Throughout the hike, Sarah had been much impressed by Mike's ability to find his way around the wilderness, but lately that had changed. She noticed him stopping to check his map more often and to take compass readings. Sometimes he would stop for ten minutes or more before deciding which way to go.

Throughout, Mike insisted that he knew precisely where he was going, and he became angered by any doubts the worried hikers expressed.

Everyone had become edgy and irritable. Sarah wanted to get the hike over with as fast as possible, but Mike increased the number of rest breaks, so that the group wouldn't become overtired in the cold weather.

As they hiked, Sarah kept looking at the front of the column where Dianne walked beside her husband. Sarah desperately wanted to talk to Dianne, but she didn't want Mike to be around when she did it. Sarah was glad when Dianne stopped to tie her boots and fell behind.

"It sure is cold," Sarah said as she stood by and watched Dianne tie her laces.

"Yeah," Dianne said. "It sure is."

She finished tying her boots and stood up.

"Let me carry your pack for a while," Sarah said.

"That's okay."

"I want to. I really do."

Dianne shrugged, then loosened the hip belt and shoulder straps and slid the pack off her back. She helped Sarah put it on; then the two women took off after the others at a hurried pace.

For a while, neither one spoke.

"I feel like shit about what happened," Sarah finally said.

Dianne looked at her and said, "Mike and I have been through this before. It wasn't your fault."

Sarah was surprised by the revelation, but didn't go into it further. She was satisfied that things were straight between her and Dianne.

For the next mile, Sarah marked the group's approach to a gray face of rock that towered above the surrounding countryside.

When they finally arrived at the base of the cliff, Mike removed his backpack and shotgun and told the others that he was going to climb to the top.

"We have to head south," he said. "I need to check my bearings."

He asked if Phil wanted to go along.

"Sure," Phil said. "Why not?"

Mike seemed delighted, but Sarah thought the idea was crazy.

"You don't know a thing about climbing," she said.

"Are you talking to me?" Phil asked.

"That's fairly obvious, isn't it?"

"I thought you weren't going to speak to me anymore."

"You're the one who wasn't speaking," Sarah said.

"We ought to get it straight who's being the asshole, don't you think?"

"If you climb that rock, there'll be no doubt about it in my mind."

"Don't worry. I'll be all right."

Phil dropped his backpack onto the ground and retied his boots while Mike gave him a few tips about climbing.

"It's an easy cliff," Mike said. "There's a good fracture line, and it's not too steep."

"Why don't you go with him?" Rachel said to Jim.

"I'll go if it's okay with Mike."

Everyone looked toward Mike to see what his response would be.

"Why not?" he said without any change in expression and acting as if nothing had passed between them.

Sarah was heartened to see things patched up between the two men. It was the first good thing to happen all day, and she hoped it was a harbinger of improved relations between everyone involved. Feelings between the hikers surely couldn't have gotten any worse.

"Let's sit down over there out of the wind," Dianne said to Sarah and Rachel. The three women went behind a large rock from where they would have a clear view of the climb.

They took off their packs and watched as the men walked up the slope of broken stone toward where the fracture line began.

"I'm surprised that Jim decided to go," Rachel said. "He drank at least a pint of gin after his scrape with Mike."

"You're kidding, aren't you?" Sarah said with surprise.

"Don't worry," Rachel laughed. "Jim's half drunk most of the time anyway. He maneuvers around pretty well."

"You should have told Mike," Dianne said. "He wouldn't have taken him."

90

Although Dianne tried her best to hide it, Sarah felt a certain stiffness in her response to Rachel. Rachel didn't answer back.

The wind was gusting even stronger as the three men climbed the first part of the cliff leading to a wide ledge where they stopped to rest before going higher. Sarah could see the men keeping their faces away from the wind, and their clothes were flapping wildly.

Jim Wheatley walked over to the edge and waved down at the women.

"What a clown," Rachel said.

The second part of the climb looked to Sarah to be harder than the first. It was steeper, and the fracture was filled with stone.

But the men worked their way to the summit with relative ease, and when they arrived at the top they celebrated the climb by passing around Jim Wheatley's flask.

Sarah watched as Mike surveyed the surrounding countryside, then finally pointed at a prominent hill in the distance that stood out plainly because there weren't any trees on the top.

After a few minutes, the men started back down through the fracture. Mike followed the others until they stopped at a point where the passage narrowed; then he moved forward as if to lead the way.

Just as he squeezed around Phil, he lost his footing. Jim lunged to catch him, but the loose stone in the fracture gave way like the melting snow on the side of a roof, and all three men came sliding down the fracture in an avalanche of rubble.

Sarah was stunned at first and watched transfixed as the mountain of rubble swallowed up the three men then crashed onto the ledge, sending up a great cloud of dust.

As soon as the reality of the scene registered, the three women raced toward the cliff, scrambling and clawing their way up to the ledge.

When they arrived, they saw a pile of debris running from one edge of the ledge to the other.

There was no sign of the men.

"They're dead," Rachel said blankly.

Dianne and Sarah charged onto the side of the pile and began digging furiously through the stone and dirt with their bare hands.

91

They moved from place to place without a hint of where they should look, when suddenly Rachel called out from the other side of the pile.

"Come here!" she screamed. "I've found one of them!"

Sarah scrambled up the loose stone to the top and leapt in great strides down the other side until she fell onto her knees where Rachel was digging.

Sarah saw an arm sticking out of the rubble, and from the shape of the hand she knew instantly that it was Phil buried underneath.

"Be careful," Sarah said. "Don't move him!"

They spent almost ten minutes pulling back the stones and dirt from around Phil's body until at last he was free. Phil remained unconscious, his face badly lacerated.

Sarah placed her hand on the side of his head and felt a huge swelling.

"I think his skull's fractured," Sarah said.

Rachel felt the spot, too. "Stay with him," she said. "I'm going to see if Jim or Mike is close by."

Dianne walked over to them slowly as if she were in a trance.

Sarah rushed to her side and, seeing how pale Dianne was, told her to lie down.

"Stay here, and don't move," Sarah ordered.

Dianne's eyes were dilated, so Sarah raised her legs onto a rock to get the blood flowing back to her brain.

With Dianne now taken care of for the moment, Sarah went back to Phil.

She gently passed her hand over his body until, coming to the right thigh, she felt an unusual lump. She noticed that his foot was turned outward and knew right away that the leg was fractured.

Although there weren't any outer signs of serious bleeding, Sarah had no idea if he had sustained any internal injuries. If he was bleeding inside, there wasn't anything she could do.

She looked around the ocean of pine trees below that stretched hill after hill as far as the eye could see.

Calm down and think, she told herself. You can't be any good to anybody unless you get hold of yourself and think clearly, and block everything else out of your mind.

She wondered whether she should move Phil or stay with him and send Rachel for help. If they were two days away from the lodge, it would take four days for help to arrive.

That's not true, Sarah thought. They could send a helicopter when Rachel makes it back. But what about the weather? With this wind, they might not be able to fly anything out.

And you don't even know which direction to go. It might take Rachel a week to find her way, and she might not find it at all, and then you'd have to sit here and watch Phil die.

While the thoughts flew chaotically through Sarah's mind, Phil suddenly began to gag.

Sarah pried his mouth open and reached as far back in his throat as her hand would go until she felt his tongue lodged in the windpipe. She pinched the tongue between her fingers and pulled it out until Phil could breathe normally again.

Rachel came back from her search and told Sarah that she was sure Mike and Jim were dead. Her tone of voice was flat.

"How's Phil doing?" she asked.

"I don't really know. I wish he would come to."

Sarah took off her parka, spread it on top of Phil, then stood up to face Rachel.

"One of us has to go for help," she said.

"Do you think we could carry Phil?"

"Even if we could, how far would we get?"

"I don't know about you, but I don't have the first idea how to get to the lodge. And Mike has the map and compass."

Sarah thought for a moment, then suddenly remembered something—it was the image of Mike Stove at the summit of the cliff.

"I think I know which way to go," she said.

"How?"

"Do you remember seeing Mike pointing over there toward that bald ridge?"

Rachel looked at the hill in question.

"Yes, I do."

"We're supposed to turn south here to get to the lodge. Mike must have been showing the way."

"I think you're right."

"There's no guarantee that it's the right direction," Sarah said. "If you want to stay here with Phil, I'll go."

"No, you stay."

"Are you sure?"

"I think I can make better time than you can."

"You're probably right. Why don't you pack up some of the food and get started right away?"

"That's no good," Rachel said. "It'll be dark soon, and I'd rather start off with plenty of daylight."

"I don't know how long Phil can make it."

"If I don't get help, he won't make it at all. My chances are better if I wait until morning."

Sarah hated the idea of delaying even by a minute any help for Phil, but she had to admit that Rachel was right. What good would it do to send Rachel off in the darkness if it meant getting lost?

"Let's get him off the mountain," Rachel said.

"He can't be moved."

"We have to move him. He'll freeze to death if he stays up here in the wind all night."

Sarah could feel the cold stiffening the muscles in her back. Even if she could pitch a tent on the mountainside, the wind would rip it to shreds or roll it off the side, with her and Phil inside.

"Okay," Sarah said reluctantly. "I'll make some splints for his leg. Why don't you check on Dianne while I'm gone."

Rachel nodded, and Sarah jogged back to the fracture line and descended the slope as quickly as she could. When she arrived at the base of the cliff, she walked back into the forest and searched for some branches that would be long enough and strong enough to make good splints. Very few of the trees had branches that came within reaching distance of the ground, and Sarah soon became discouraged. Finally she discovered a huge pine tree with whirls of dead branches all around the trunk.

She tried to break off one of the branches but found it too sturdy, so she had to run back and get Mike Stove's bow saw to complete the job.

With two poles now in hand, she returned to the cliff as fast as she could, stopping only briefly to get some cloth bandages from Mike's pack. Then she threaded her way back up the slope and returned to Phil's side.

Rachel came over to join her, leaving Dianne among the rubble.

"Dianne's totally out of it," Rachel said.

94

"Keep an eye on her. I don't want her walking off the side of the cliff."

Sarah placed one of the poles, the longer of the two, along Phil's right side, so it extended from below the heel all the way to the top of his head. Then she placed the shorter of the two poles along the inside of his leg from the groin to below the heel.

With the splints in place, Sarah tore up the bandages into shorter strips and tied them around both poles the entire length of the leg, then used bigger strips to tie the longer pole around his torso up to his armpits.

"That should do it," Sarah said as she tied the last knot.

It felt good to be able to do something useful. If she stayed busy, and concentrated only on doing things right, she could stay in control and keep out all the feelings that would make her as useless as Dianne.

"It's the head injury I'm most worried about," she said, standing up now.

"Why don't you pick him up under the arms, and I'll take his legs?"

"No, we need a stretcher of some kind. In first aid class they showed us how to make one with a blanket, but we don't have any blankets."

"How about the sleeping bags?"

"Good idea," Sarah said excitedly. "Stay here!"

Again she descended the cliff. She went back to the giant pine and sawed off two large branches; then she untied Jim Wheatley's sleeping bag from his pack frame and brought everything back up the hill with her.

"He looks really bad," Rachel said when Sarah returned.

She pointed toward some clear fluid leaking from Phil's ear.

"Do you see that? What does it mean?"

"It's something to do with the head injury," Sarah said.

Sarah lifted her sweater at the bottom and reached for the snap on her sheath. She took out Mike's knife and proceeded to cut out the bottom corners of the sleeping bag.

When the holes were open, she slid the two branches down both sides of the bag until they popped through the holes and stuck out a couple feet on either side.

"Okay," she said. "We have to lift him very carefully. We could make things even worse."

Sarah placed the makeshift stretcher next to Phil and

told Rachel to kneel alongside her. Then they painstakingly rolled him onto his side, Sarah cradling his head, and moved the stretcher closer. Finally, they rolled him back onto the sleeping bag and centered him.

"Good," Sarah said.

She had been concentrating so hard on not hurting Phil that she was wet with perspiration.

"I'm going to bring Dianne down first," Sarah said. "We can't leave her up here alone."

"I think she'll be all right."

"I don't want to take the chance."

While Rachel stayed with Phil, Sarah walked over to where Dianne was lying on the ground. Dianne's color remained poor. She was ghastly white.

"Do you think you can stand up?" Sarah asked her.

Dianne looked up at her without recognition.

"Come with me."

"I want to go home," Dianne said. "I want to go home with Mike."

"Okay, come with me, and I'll take you home."

Dianne took hold of Sarah's hands and stood up. Then she passively followed Sarah back to the fracture line and continued to hold on to her hand until they reached the bottom.

Sarah led her over to the backpacks, out of the wind, and spread an ensolite pad on the ground.

"Lie down," she told Dianne, "and wait until I get back."

"I want to go home," Dianne said again.

"I'll take you home as soon as I get back." Dianne mechanically lay down on the pad and rested her head on a sweater. Sarah unstrapped Mike's sleeping bag and placed it under Dianne's legs to elevate them.

The forest was getting dark fast. Sarah told Dianne to lie still; then she rushed back to Phil and Rachel.

"You take the front of the stretcher," she told Rachel.

"How can we get down without using our hands?"

"I don't know, but we have to try."

The two women lifted the stretcher, and, when Sarah was confident that it would hold Phil, they moved slowly back to the fracture and inched their way down the steep drop.

Each step had to be taken carefully. The passage was more dangerous because the rockslide had covered the path with loose stone, and it was difficult to tell which stones were solid.

"He's rolling off!" Sarah shouted, yanking the stretcher sharply the other way. "Pick up the left side!"

They managed to catch Phil just before he fell.

"Keep him level," Sarah yelled.

"I can't do that and see where the hell I'm going."

Sarah's arms were aching from the constant tension. She couldn't see where she was putting her feet with the stretcher in the way.

She stumbled and fell onto her knee, but managed to keep the stretcher up.

"I'm okay," she yelled to Rachel. "Keep going."

It took a painfully long time, but they finally reached the bottom of the cliff and placed Phil down next to Dianne.

While they sat and caught their breath, Sarah stared at the side of the cliff as if she were trying to make it real in her mind.

"It'll be dark soon," Rachel said. "We'd better make camp."

"It's too rocky here," Sarah said. "I'll look around for a better spot."

Rachel nodded, and Sarah got up and headed down a gradual slope in the forest where it looked like there weren't as many rocks.

She was ready to turn back and look somewhere else when she noticed a level area of ground just uphill from an outcrop of rock.

It was smooth and large enough for the tents. With the growing dark, it would have to do.

"I found a good place," she told Rachel when she got back up the hill. "It's not very far."

"Dianne won't even talk to me," Rachel said. "She won't be any use to us at all."

Sarah knelt by Dianne's side and spoke softly.

"Do you think you can walk to the campsite?" she asked.

Dianne said that she wasn't sure.

"Let's give it a try," Sarah said.

Sarah helped Dianne stand up; then, holding her under her arm, she led her slowly down the hillside to a flat rock, where she told her to sit down.

"Wait for me," Sarah said. "I'll be back in a minute."

When Sarah returned to Rachel, they put on their backpacks, then picked up the stretcher and brought Phil to the campsite.

Only the nearest trees were visible as they set Phil down.

"I'll get the other packs," Rachel said.

"Good. I'll set up Phil's tent while you're gone."

As Sarah unpacked the tent and assembled the poles, she realized that something had changed in the forest—the wind had stopped.

The silence was scary.

By the time Sarah had erected the tent and pulled the fly over the top, Rachel returned with the packs and shotgun, and together the two women hastily set up the other two tents in a tight row that completely filled the level site.

"I'm going to make a fire," Rachel said. "The wind has died down enough."

Sarah had disliked the darkness in the forest on previous nights, and tonight she disliked it even more. A bright, warm fire would be welcome.

Before the fire could be built, they had to bring Phil to his tent. It was a difficult move getting him inside without dragging him on the ground, and it took several minutes of careful maneuvering.

They made sure that his head was elevated slightly higher than the rest of his body, so that they wouldn't aggravate any bleeding under his skull.

Once he was settled in the tent and warmly bundled up, Rachel took Mike Stove's bow saw back into the trees to look for wood while Sarah cleaned the wounds on Phil's face.

By the time she was finished dressing the cuts with antiseptic powder and bandaging them with gauze and tape, she could see the light of the fire against the tent.

Sarah went back outside and joined Rachel and Dianne.

There wasn't anything said for a while. Dianne and Sarah stared into the flames while Rachel stacked up wood nearby.

"Do you want anything to eat?" Rachel asked.

Sarah said no. Dianne wasn't paying attention.

"But go ahead," Sarah said. "You'll need your strength."

As soon as Rachel went to her backpack for food, Dianne turned to Sarah, her face ashen, and said that she didn't feel well.

Sarah got up and held Dianne's shoulders just as she turned her head aside and began to vomit.

"It's okay," Sarah said as she comforted Dianne.

Dianne had the dry heaves for a while, then turned to look at Sarah. Her eyes were watery and red.

"You should go to bed," Sarah said. "Come on. Let me help you."

Dianne nodded okay, and together she and Sarah walked to the tent and crawled inside. Sarah helped Dianne take off her parka and boots, then zipped her inside her sleeping bag.

She went back outside momentarily to get a pan from one of the cook sets. Then she returned and set the pan near Dianne's head.

"You can use this if you have to," Sarah said.

She brushed the hair from Dianne's face.

"I'll come back to check on you. If you need anything, just yell."

She pulled the sleeping bag under Dianne's chin, then left the tent and stood up.

As soon as she did, she saw Rachel staring into the forest.

"Listen!" Rachel said.

At last, Sarah heard something—it was a soft crunching in the dried pine needles on the ground.

"What do you think it is?" Sarah asked Rachel.

"I don't know, but it's headed this way."

Sarah got the flashlight from Phil's pack and directed it into the darkness. All she saw was the dark outline of trees.

"It sounds close," she said. "Why can't we see it?"

"Whatever it is, we're going to be ready for it," Rachel said.

While Sarah looked on, Rachel went to Mike's backpack and untied his shotgun. She took the gun over by the fire and loaded the receiver with three shells.

"Where'd you learn how to do that?" Sarah asked.

Rachel pumped the forearm with a sharp snap.

"Mike showed me," she said.

She walked up next to Sarah and told her to shine the flashlight in a scanning motion from left to right while she aimed the gun and followed it.

"Can you hear anything?" Rachel asked.

"It's moving over there."

They listened as the crunching sound came closer toward

them. Rachel aimed the shotgun toward the spot while Sarah held the flashlight.

"I think it's a bear," Sarah said.

"It can't be a bear."

"Why can't it?"

"I don't know. It just isn't."

"Then it must be a deer."

"That's right, it's a deer, and I'm going to blow its head off if it comes near us."

Sarah was still convinced it was a bear.

"Let's try to scare it away," she said.

"How?"

"This is how."

Suddenly Sarah started screaming and continued to scream until she was out of breath.

Finally there was silence; then, a moment later, they heard whatever was out there moving back up the hillside.

"It was a bear," Sarah said. "I'm sure it was."

Rachel took the shells out of the shotgun and put them back in the pack. She leaned the gun against a tree close to the tents.

With the immediate scare now over, the sad reality of the afternoon returned.

It was hard for Sarah to concentrate on what needed to be done.

"Maybe you should try to go back to the lodge the way we came," Sarah told Rachel.

"Do you remember how to get back?"

"No."

"I don't either. Heading for the bald ridge is a safer bet. I know that Mike was pointing there."

"How early can you leave?"

"As soon as it gets light."

"It might be a good idea to mark your path so you can come back if things don't work out."

"They'll work out."

"Let's divide up the rest of the food before we go to bed," Sarah said.

"Good idea. That way I can leave right away tomorrow."

"And don't forget to bring a stove and flint."

"I won't."

"With the wind gone, it should be a lot easier to stay warm."

"I hope it stays that way."

"I wish to hell I could do more for Phil. If only he would wake up, I'd feel a lot better."

"What will you do if I don't make it to the lodge?"

"Don't even say that."

"You have to come up with a plan, even if you never have to use it."

"I guess that Dianne and I will try to carry Phil."

"You'd never make it."

"What else can I do?"

"You're not going to like this, but it's the only sensible thing."

"You think that I should leave Phil behind, don't you?"

"That's right."

"I couldn't do that."

"You might not have any choice."

"Bob Harwood is sure to miss us after a while."

"Harwood said that he was going away for a couple of weeks," Rachel said.

"Then someone will miss us at work."

"Nobody misses me at work. Besides, it could be too late."

"Dianne's folks are taking care of her kids. They're bound to wonder what happened."

"Dianne told me that her parents took the kids to their place at the shore for two weeks so Dianne and Mike could spend some time at home alone."

"We can always go hunting with Mike's shotgun," Sarah said. "We'd have enough food to last a long time then."

"It's not likely we'd get anything."

"How many days would I wait for you to come back?"

"If I were you, I'd try to walk out after four days . . . five at the most. And don't go in the same direction that I do."

"Let's hope it doesn't come to that."

"It probably won't, but, if it does, don't let Phil and Dianne stop you from saving your own life."

"I could never leave them," Sarah said.

"You'll feel differently when the hunger pains start."

Sarah didn't answer.

They stayed by the fire awhile longer, then brought all the backpacks together and emptied out the food. Rachel let Sarah divide the provisions, and she appeared satisfied with the results.

When they were finished, they brought their packs into the woods and tied them up in a tree with nylon rope.

Sarah put out the fire by kicking dirt onto it; then she followed Rachel to the tents. She was just about to say goodnight when Rachel turned to her and said, "By the way, I want you to know that I didn't burn Jim's novel. He burned it himself."

Before Sarah could say anything, Rachel slipped into her tent, leaving Sarah alone in the dark.

Sarah thought the timing of the revelation was especially queer, but she was too tired to give it any attention. Before turning in, she went to check on Dianne.

She found her crying softly.

"Do you want anything?" Sarah asked.

Dianne didn't answer.

"I'm going to bed," Sarah said, "but I'll be right next door if you need me."

Sarah slipped her hand inside Dianne's sleeping bag to make sure that her canteen was still there, so that the water wouldn't freeze overnight.

"It's important for you to drink," Sarah told her.

It was like talking to a stone. Sarah patted Dianne's shoulder reassuringly, then turned around and crawled outside. She zipped up the tent flaps and went to her own tent.

On the way over, she noticed that there wasn't any moon or stars in the sky. It was still cloudy. At least the wind had stopped, and she was thankful for that.

When she went inside her tent and turned on the flashlight, she saw that Phil was still unconscious. She put her hand inside the neck of his parka to make sure he was warm.

Then she moved her ensolite pad and sleeping bag close alongside, put her canteen inside, and undressed. She slid into her sleeping bag and trembled slightly as she waited for the bag to warm. It took a long time.

As she lay in the dark, she listened to Phil's labored breathing. Sometimes he would stop breathing altogether, and Sarah would try to breathe for him.

It made it impossible to go to sleep.

Sarah thought how strange it was that she knew Phil intimately, and yet now his body was a terrifying stranger. She imagined herself waking up and finding him dead.

Sarah kept thinking that she should be home in New York washing out her nylons and wondering whether to make her lunch or eat out and blow the budget.

If she died, it was supposed to be because of a car accident or a mugging or breast cancer, not freezing to death out in the middle of the wilderness.

Sarah was obsessed with the haunting images of the accident—the rockslide crashing onto the ledge, the first sight of Phil's lacerated hand sticking from the rubble, Dianne's pitiful expression when she finally stopped digging for Mike and knew he was dead.

Sarah was glad that Rachel was the one who would try to hike to the lodge. She was tougher and stronger.

She was a survivor.

Close your eyes now and go to sleep, Sarah told herself. Things will work out. They always do.

She wished she could wake up in the morning and find herself under the covers with Phil, with an empty champagne bottle next to the bed, and know that everything had been a silly dream.

But her aching legs and the acrid smell of urine from Phil's sleeping bag were no dream.

Go to sleep, she told herself. Stop thinking and let the tiredness take over.

As she huddled up next to Phil, placing her knee against his hip and burying her head under the top of the sleeping bag, she wondered why the air smelled different tonight.

Day Five

All of Sarah's nightmares that night concerned suffocation. She was locked in a dark closet with her cat. She was trapped beneath the ice. She was buried alive by an avalanche of rock.

She awoke with a start and looked at Phil. He hadn't moved an inch. She quickly reached her hand over and felt his throat for a pulse.

It was there—strong and regular. His breathing sounded normal.

Sarah looked at her watch and was surprised that it was after eight.

Why was it so dark? Why did the air feel muffled?

She unzipped her bag and pulled herself out; then she put on her parka and boots before unzipping the flaps to the tent.

Much to her surprise, a mound of snow tumbled inside.

She stuck her head outside and looked over the drift in front of the tent. The branches of a nearby fir tree were heavy with snow, and the flakes were falling so thick in the air that she could barely see up the side of the hill.

As soon as she crawled out and stood up, she noticed that Rachel's tent was gone. There was a depression in the snow where it had been sitting, but new snow had almost covered it up.

Sarah's first reaction was fear, but then she told herself that it didn't really matter that Rachel had left early, as long as she made it to the lodge.

Still, it was strange that Rachel had left without saying good-bye.

Dianne's tent was burdened with snow, the walls sagging greatly. Sarah brushed off some of the snow, then kicked away the pile in front of the flaps and went inside.

Dianne was curled up in her sleeping bag, bleary-eyed but wide awake.

"Did Rachel say anything to you before she left?" Sarah asked.

Dianne rolled over and looked at Sarah blankly.

"Why would she?"

"She went to the lodge to get help," Sarah said.

"It's too late for that."

"We have to talk about what we're going to do while she's gone," Sarah said.

"I don't care."

"I know how you must feel, but we need to plan."

"Leave me alone, will you? I don't care. I just don't care!"

Sarah decided not to push things for the moment, but she hoped that Dianne would get over her black mood soon, at least enough to be of some help.

"Okay," Sarah said, "but we're going to talk later."

Dianne didn't say anything, and Sarah left the tent.

She walked back into the trees where they had strung up their backpacks the evening before. As expected, Rachel's pack was gone. But, when Sarah lowered her own pack and looked inside, she found something that she hadn't expected—most of her food was gone.

"Damn her to hell!" she said aloud as she rummaged through the pack, hoping that some of the food had fallen into the bottom.

It hadn't.

Sarah quickly took out all the packages and counted them once, twice, and three times. Then she divided the total by the food they would consume each day.

Four lousy days! she said angrily. We had enough for a week, and now there's only four lousy, rotten days!

She glanced off into the forest and thought of chasing after Rachel to get back the food.

It's no use, she told herself. Rachel's got too much of a head start, and the snow will have covered her trail.

Sarah was both scared and furious as she carried the pack of remaining food and closed it up inside her tent next to Phil. She picked up Mike's bow saw and went off into the trees to get some wood for a fire.

No wonder Rachel was so confident about making it to the lodge, she thought. The shitbird stole enough food to last a month!

Sarah brought back an armful of kindling to the campsite and made a small tepee of branches over balls of wax-paper. Luckily the snow was dry and powdery, so the wood was dry, too. She lit the paper with a stick match, and, as soon as the tepee was burning, she took the bow saw back into the woods to find more fuel.

When she couldn't find anything large enough on the ground, she decided to cut down a dead pine tree. She sawed the tree on the uphill side, so that it would fall down below her.

As she knelt in the deep snow, sawing back and forth, she tried to reassure herself.

You've got to believe that Rachel will make it, she thought. If she does, it won't make any difference what she did to you.

The tree cracked, and Sarah quickly stepped back to watch it fall. Then she dragged it to the campsite, and, after removing the branches and placing them on the fire, she went to work cutting the trunk into logs.

When she was done, Sarah stood over the fire awhile warming her hands; then she lit up Phil's stove and boiled some water for hot cereal.

As she waited for the oatmeal to cook, she looked around the wintry landscape and wondered why Mike had been so worried about the prospect of snow.

It seemed harmless enough. In fact, the weather was warmer than yesterday now that the wind was gone. And the wilderness snow wasn't slushy and sooty like city snow. It brushed away easily like Styrofoam, and when you walked through it there was good traction.

As Sarah stirred the oatmeal, she heard something inside her tent. She went to investigate and found Phil trying to sit up.

"Stay still!" she told him.

His eyes were heavy. He could barely keep them open.

"What happened?" he asked weakly.

"There was an accident. You broke your leg, but you're going to be okay."

"I want to talk to Mike," he said.

"Mike's not here right now."

Phil appeared satisfied with the answer. His eyelids were drooping, and Sarah knew she didn't have much time to talk.

"Listen closely," she said. "I have to know if Mike was going to take us to the bald hill."

Phil grimaced from the pain in his leg.

"Can you hear me, Phil?"

He nodded, then licked his cracked lips and said in a whisper, "Go to the hill. Then south through the meadows."

It was all that Sarah could get out of him because Phil closed his eyes and went unconscious again.

What meadows? Sarah thought. What does that mean?

She covered Phil, then left the tent and looked up the hill through the trees and the heavy snow at the cliff.

She knew that there was only one way to find out what Phil had meant, and that was to hike to the meadows and have a look for herself.

Before leaving, she ate the hot oatmeal and then stopped by to tell Dianne what she was up to, so she wouldn't worry about her.

Dianne ignored her completely.

Sarah went outside and got her canteen from the tent. Then she wrapped her face in a scarf and marched up the hill toward the cliff.

When she arrived at the base, she looked out across the frozen countryside and immediately spotted the bald hill with its white peak.

She guessed that it would take half an hour to walk there, but she wasn't sure of the distance.

The rest of the forest looked gray and bleak, despite the heavy snow.

Before going back to the campsite, Sarah looked up the side of the cliff at the rockslide where Jim and Mike were buried. The snow had covered the rubble with a white shroud, wiping out any trace of the previous day's tragedy.

The hike to the bald hill was slow but relatively easy. The snow kicked aside like talcum powder. Sarah stayed in the hollows and arrived at the hill some twenty minutes after she had started out.

The slope was steep in some parts, and Sarah had to rest a few times on the way up. The hill was covered with gnarled and rotted trees. Sarah thought that maybe disease had killed them, but when she saw some blackened stumps sticking out from the snow, she knew there must have been a fire. Already, hundreds of saplings were springing up to replace the burned trees, many of them growing right out of the side of the stumps.

When Sarah reached the top of the hill, she walked across the open knoll until she could look out over the countryside below. The meadows that Phil talked about were clearly visible, as if someone had poured white paint between the hills.

She knew that if she headed straight through the meadows, she would come to the river in a day, and the lodge would be only one day beyond that.

But, turning around to head back, Sarah realized at once that Rachel was walking in the wrong direction. The cliff should have been directly in front of her, but instead it was way off to the left.

To make certain, Sarah broke off a twig and made a map in the snow like the one Mike had shown her back at the lodge. She drew the half circle and the river, then drew a straight line that passed between the cliff and the bald hill.

The conclusion was obvious—if Rachel kept going straight, then she would miss the river entirely and never come close to the lodge.

For the first time since the accident, Sarah felt totally stranded in the middle of the vast countryside. Until now, her knowledge that Rachel was trekking to the lodge for help had been like a link to civilization, but now the link was broken.

As Sarah turned around and headed back down the hill, she pondered her options.

You can stay here, she thought, and hope that someone misses you or that Rachel runs into something, and that all this happens before you starve or freeze to death. Or you can take some of the food and try to get to the lodge on your own and hope that Dianne will take care of herself and Phil while you're gone.

That won't work, Sarah thought. Dianne won't even feed herself. She's too much in shock about what happened to think of anything else. If you leave her alone with Phil, she might just walk off into the forest.

As Sarah followed her own tracks through the snow, she went over all the tangibles again—how much food they had left, how many days they could stretch it out by strict rationing. But whenever she pictured herself waiting for help to arrive while the food slowly ran out and Phil grew progressively worse, her instincts recoiled from the notion. There was something too dangerously passive about sitting back and hoping that someone would miraculously come by to save them.

Above everything else, Sarah felt she had to do something. The hike to the bald-topped hill was infinitely better than sitting at camp. The only times she was unafraid were when she could focus her attention on action and concentrate on it entirely.

When Sarah made it back to the campsite, the fire was going out, and Dianne was still inside her tent, staring at the walls as if she were resigned to stare at them for the rest of her life.

Sarah tried to talk to her about some of the realities they were facing, but Dianne seemed uninterested in her own survival.

All of this impressed Sarah once again with the impossibility of leaving Dianne behind to take care of Phil.

Dianne was as helpless as a little child. There was only one way to deal with her.

"Get dressed and go outside," Sarah said firmly. "I'll meet you by the fire."

Dianne looked up at her a moment, puzzled, then obediently unzipped her sleeping bag.

Sarah left the tent and returned to Phil. His face was flushed with fever, and Sarah became more convinced than ever that he would die unless he got help soon.

She knew it wasn't good to move him, and she knew that it would be hard if not impossible to carry him all the way to the lodge, but she couldn't think of any other alternative.

It's worth a try, she told herself. You can take it one step at a time, and if it all falls apart you can still pitch the tent and go back to what you're doing now, which is absolutely nothing and will get you absolutely nowhere but dead.

Sarah slid the two stretcher poles back into the sides of the sleeping bag and made certain that Phil's splints were well-tied and that he was covered. His sleeping bag was damp with urine, but Sarah knew that the Polar Guard filling would keep him warm even though it was wet, and his wool clothes would do the same.

When Phil was ready to be moved, Sarah called outside for Dianne to come and help. They pulled him gently from inside the tent and set him down in the snow.

"Pack up," Sarah told Dianne.

"Why?"

"We're going to hike back to the lodge."

"I want to stay here and wait for Rachel to get help."

"Rachel isn't going to get help. She's walking the wrong way."

"How do you know?"

"I just know. Now pack up. I want to get started right away."

For a moment it looked like Dianne was going to balk, but then, without a word, she went to her tent and started taking it down.

Sarah was greatly relieved to see that Dianne could be moved to action by direct commands. She needed Dianne's help.

Sarah gathered together the rest of the backpacks and dumped everything out on a poncho. Then she carefully selected just what they needed for the hike to the lodge. She guessed that it would take three days; that would give them one day longer than it would normally take, and it wouldn't be fatal if it took them four days or even five, because they had just barely enough food.

Sarah decided to leave behind the clothing and two of the tents because they would only make it more difficult to carry the stretcher. She would keep all the food, one stove, one tent, three sleeping bags, sufficient cookware and utensils to eat with, a flint, some stick matches in a waterproof canister, and all three ponchos.

And the gun, too. She could fire it off once in a while as a distress signal.

Sarah placed the shotgun alongside the stretcher and tied it with short pieces of rope. She found two boxes of shells in Mike's backpack, one of them marked "buckshot," the other "rifle slug." She didn't know what "buck" meant, so she took the rifle slugs.

Finally, she stuffed the rest of the gear and provisions into the backpacks that she and Dianne would wear while carrying the stretcher.

When everything was organized, and the tent and sleeping bags were strapped to the pack frames, and the fire was put out with snow, Sarah looked at Mike and Jim's gutted backpacks and felt more immediately than ever before that the two men were really dead and would not be returning home.

Sarah quickly fought off the emotion.

Before leaving camp, she took out a red flannel shirt belonging to Jim Wheatley and left a note in the pocket telling what direction they would be heading. Then she tied the shirt onto a branch where it would be clearly visible to anyone passing by.

"Let's go," she said to Dianne.

They lifted the stretcher—Sarah in front and Dianne behind—and they started their way slowly up the hillside toward the cliff.

When they reached the clearing at the base, Sarah looked around until she recognized the route to the bald-topped hill. They put Phil down and rested before continuing.

"We're going to take it very slowly," Sarah said to Dianne as they headed into the treeline. "But, if you can't hold on, tell me, and we'll rest."

The snow continued to fall heavily, and Sarah's tracks from her previous hike were already covered up. The air was perfectly still, and the only sound was the soft crunching of their boots in the snow.

Sarah found the stretcher somewhat lighter than she had expected and was heartened. She kept telling herself they could make it to the lodge if they tackled the distance in manageable pieces.

When they arrived at the bald hill, Sarah checked her watch and saw that it had taken them an hour and a half to get there. If they kept up that pace, she figured that it would take them five days to get to the lodge. It wasn't good news, but Sarah thought they could live with it if they were careful with the food reserves.

Sarah left Dianne and Phil to reclimb the hill and assure herself of her bearings to the meadows.

When she returned she rested awhile; then they picked up the stretcher and started hiking south.

Keeping on course was easy as they went through the meadows, but Sarah knew that it would be harder once they re-entered the forest, where everything looked the same. Sarah stopped for a minute when they reached the end of the meadows and looked back at the bald-topped hill with the cliff looming behind it. Then she turned straight around and targeted two trees that were in line.

"Okay," she told Dianne. "Let's go."

They picked up Phil again and walked slowly into the forest, Sarah pinning her eyes on the chosen markers. As she neared the closer tree, she sighted up a third in line with the other two and continued the process.

It was a difficult trick for the first hour. Sarah usually had to stop walking and burned up a lot of time in the process, but with practice she got better and could line up recognizable trees by their shape or branches, and she could do it without losing a step.

At noontime Sarah decided to stop a full hour, even though she knew their progress was much slower than she had hoped it would be.

After building a small fire and placing Phil near it, she untied Mike's shotgun from the stretcher and loaded it the way she had seen Rachel do it the night before.

She pumped the forearm, then aimed the gun high into the sky. With some trepidation, she squeezed the trigger.

Nothing happened.

She squinted her eyes and tried to fire the gun once again.

Still nothing.

Sarah swore aloud as she examined the gun to see what was wrong. She was about to give up when she noticed the safety catch and removed it.

This time, when she fired the gun, it went off and almost took her shoulder off in the process. The explosion boomed out across the countryside.

Sarah was stunned by the kick of the gun and was reluctant to try and fire it again. But the second time she held the butt much tighter against her shoulder, and when the gun fired it didn't hurt.

Sarah listened a minute or two for a response to her signals, but there was no reply.

Sarah tied the gun back on the stretcher, then got out some food for lunch. She tried to get Dianne to eat, but Dianne spent the entire hour staring off into the woods.

Phil continued to run a fever, and Sarah was afraid he was becoming dehydrated. If he would wake up, she could force him to drink.

After the break, they started on their way again, but the long rest didn't help very much. For the first time, Dianne complained that she was tired and cold and wanted to make camp.

Sarah refused to stop.

That afternoon the wind picked up sharply and started blowing the snow into their faces, making it harder for Sarah to see her markers.

She tried to stay in the hollows the way Mike had done, but the snow was piling up too deep there, so she moved up onto the hillsides where the snow wasn't as deep.

They were cutting across a particularly steep hillside when Dianne stumbled, and Phil rolled off the stretcher, tumbling down the hill a few yards. Sarah ran to his side and rolled him over to see if he was hurt. His face was covered with snow, and she brushed it off.

"Get down here!" Sarah yelled at Dianne.

Dianne slowly dragged the stretcher over.

"You could have killed him, dammit. What the hell's the matter with you?"

She yanked the stretcher from Dianne's hands and placed it next to Phil. She carefully rolled him back onto it, then covered him up again.

"I can't walk anymore," Dianne said.

"Oh, shut up."

"I really can't."

Sarah stood up and grabbed Dianne's shoulders.

"I'm not going to die out here," she said, "and you and Phil aren't going to die either. And the reason none of us is going to die is because you're going to stop your goddamn whining and do what I tell you to do!"

Dianne started to cry.

"Stop it," Sarah said.

She shook Dianne hard, but the crying continued. Completely frustrated by the wind and the snow and the disappointing lack of progress carrying Phil, Sarah threw Dianne to the ground.

At last she stopped crying.

"Help me pick him up," Sarah said in a subdued voice.

She gave Dianne her hand and lifted her to her feet. Then, in silence, the two women picked up the stretcher and started once again alongside the hill.

As the afternoon dragged, the rest breaks grew longer and more frequent. Sarah was discouraged to the point of tears, but she was too tired to cry.

The rushing wind, the swirl of snow, the sheer boredom of the march lulled her into reverie. Her mind drifted back to memories of other snows in different times.

She remembered the hours she spent watching her brother and his friends challenge the most notorious sledding hill in the neighborhood.

Sarah would revel in Jason's glory when he successfully maneuvered the slope, sailed over the moguls, and rocketed headlong toward the chain link fence by the highway, where he had to throw himself off the sled at the last possible moment before crashing.

There were never any girls on the slope.

Sarah also remembered the snowstorm in which they buried her father and how things quickly unraveled afterward. Her mother became ill and suffered a paralyzing stroke. Jason took over the family chemical business, but soon lost most of the accounts, so he moved to Oregon with his wife and children to start a new life.

Sarah was glad that her father never lived to see the divorce. He and Gary were best of friends. They went to hockey games together, drank together, and teased her together.

Within a year of the funeral, Sarah's marriage began to show terminal symptoms. Gary escaped into his schoolwork and no longer wanted to do anything with her . . . including make love. He was always too tired or too busy.

Sarah let the situation slide, hoping that it would go away when Gary graduated in a few months, but, when she discovered that he was sleeping with another med student one week before graduation, she threw him out of the apartment.

"I was going to leave you anyway," Gary said. "You've become a real bore."

Gary left, but his credit card bills kept rolling in, and it was a hopeless battle to get him to pay up. Even the old car began to fall apart. It was in the garage more than it was out, and Sarah had to borrow money to pay the repair bills.

One day Sarah returned to the apartment to find that Gary had stolen the stereo and tape deck. He left a note saying that the equipment was rightly his.

It was true. Sarah had bought it for him to celebrate their wedding anniversary.

New York became an entirely different city once she was on her own. Without Gary around, there was no wall of protection. Kooks lurked everywhere; she had never noticed them all before, and it seemed like they were holding a convention along the route between the subway station and her apartment.

In the middle of her depression, Sarah met Phil. He was kind and concerned. He made her laugh for the first time in months.

Phil was great at taking care of the dirty work in Sarah's life. He enjoyed doing everything for her. He got her finances in order, found a lawyer to handle the divorce, and even lent her money for a new car.

Life was much easier with Phil around. Did it matter that she wasn't really in love with him?

A muffled booming sound yanked Sarah from her reverie.

"What was that?" Dianne asked.

"I'm not sure. I think it might have been a gun."

They listened again, and the second time there was no doubt.

"Put down the stretcher!" Sarah shouted.

As soon as Phil was down, Sarah ran off in the direction of the shots, yelling over her shoulder for Dianne to stay with Phil.

She struggled to run through the deep snow, but it was like running in the shallow end of a swimming pool.

After burning up all her energy, Sarah fell headfirst into a drift and started to cry. Her legs felt like they were made of lead. She could no longer lift them. Totally drained from her run, Sarah cried uncontrollably as she lay with her face buried in the snow, wishing she could die and be done with it.

Her face was numb from the snow as she got back on her feet and tried to gather her feelings.

Suddenly she remembered the shotgun.

Angry at herself for having missed the opportunity to signal the hunters, Sarah tried to jog back through the deep snow, knowing that each passing minute meant that the hunters would be farther away.

Her legs were cramping terribly as she made it back to the others and went for the gun. She loaded three rounds in the receiver and fired them off in rapid succession, pumping the forearm, making the countryside echo with the booming sound of the gun.

When she stopped, all she could hear was the wind blowing through the pine trees.

Sarah threw the shotgun in the snow and looked at Dianne, who was standing motionless next to the stretcher, her expression pitiably forlorn.

I'll take care of you, Sarah thought to herself with a tired resolve. I'll take care of you and Phil and the whole goddamn human race.

"It's okay," she tried to assure Dianne. "We'll find them."

Sarah walked to Dianne and hugged her tightly.

With the snow falling as hard as ever, they lifted Phil and started hiking once again along the side of the hill.

Sarah was aware that she was pushing herself and pushing Dianne, but she was set on going as far as they could before stopping for the day. She knew that their progress was slower than she had hoped it would be, and she feared that her estimate of five days to the lodge was overly optimistic.

For every five minutes they walked with the stretcher, they would rest for ten, and even at that pace Dianne complained bitterly. Sarah was greatly surprised when, at the end of one of the breaks, Dianne began to explain how buyer's and seller's points work in real estate.

"Why are you telling me this?" Sarah said.

"Because you really should buy a house in Jersey. It's much smarter than renting."

"Are you serious?"

"There are a lot of tax advantages to home ownership."

"I'll keep that in mind if we get out of here."

They had started hiking again when Sarah thought she heard Dianne giggling behind her.

"What are you laughing about?" she asked, turning around to look at Dianne.

Dianne's eyes were filled with tears. She was laughing and shivering so hard that she could barely hold on to the stretcher.

Sarah recognized the signs of hypothermia.

Remembering what Mike Stove had taught her, she took off her backpack, unstrapped her sleeping bag, and spread it out on the snow. She led Dianne over to the bag and had her get inside with all her clothes on. Then Sarah went off to look for a level spot of ground where they could spend the night.

She soon found a place among some outcrops of rock and

117

kicked the snow out of the way so she could set up the tent. She ran back to her pack, brought it to the nearby sight, and set up the tent, fumbling with the poles in her haste.

Since it was only about fifty feet to the campsite, Sarah dragged Dianne the distance to the tent and then pulled her inside.

Then she went back to Phil and shoved an ensolite pad underneath the stretcher to keep him warm while she took care of Dianne. The falling snow piled up quickly, so Sarah covered Phil with a poncho and anchored it with some stones.

Assured that Phil was protected from the elements, Sarah went back to the tent.

Dianne continued to shiver uncontrollably. Sarah unzipped the sleeping bag, got inside next to her, and held her tightly, but even after several minutes the sleeping bag remained cold.

Then she realized that their parkas were keeping the heat from transferring, so she quickly took them off and tried again.

This time it worked. Sarah felt the first flush of warmth pass between them.

Eventually Dianne's violent shaking subsided into milder spasms. And she was breathing much more easily. Sarah waited until she was sure that Dianne was out of danger; then she got out of the sleeping bag and left the tent to make some hot tea.

She removed the stove from the backpack, pumped it up, and lit it with the flint. She put on a pan of water, then went back to Phil to see if he was all right.

She took the poncho off him and felt his neck. The pulse was strong and regular. She took hold of the ends of the sleeping bag and carefully dragged Phil through the snow over to the campsite. Then she pulled him into the tent alongside Dianne, who was curled up inside her sleeping bag with her eyes closed.

At last Sarah could catch her breath. She knelt down in front of the tent on one knee and tried to slow everything down.

She realized how stupid she had been to keep pushing Dianne when she was exhausted and refused to eat or drink. It was like trying to run a furnace without any fuel.

Tired and dejected, Sarah dragged herself to her feet

and walked slowly to the stove, where the water she had left on was steaming into the cold air. Sarah got a cup from her backpack, made some tea, and brought it to Dianne.

"Here," she said. "Drink this."

"What is it?"

"Hot tea. It will be good for you."

Dianne picked herself up on her elbow and drank sparingly.

"How do you feel?" Sarah asked.

"I've never been so weak in my life."

Sarah reached in her pocket for a granola bar she kept there to snack on while she was hiking.

"You should eat this," Sarah said. "You haven't had anything all day."

Dianne ate the crumbling bar slowly and without any enthusiasm.

Sarah wanted her to eat more, but it was difficult to force someone else to eat when you didn't feel like eating yourself.

More than anything else, Sarah was tired. It was the kind of tired where she could easily have keeled over without undressing, fallen asleep instantly, and slept forever. She was too tired to think, but thinking was what she most needed to do at the moment.

Exhausted to the point of uselessness, Sarah managed to remember the food and how stupid it would be to leave it on the ground overnight, where any animal could get it.

She was encouraged that she had remembered the food because it meant that she was still in control and wasn't letting the crucial things slip by.

She dragged herself from the tent and took the nylon rope from the side pocket of her backpack. Then she tied a stone to the rope and tossed it over the highest branch she could reach. She pulled the backpack up to the branch, but, worried that a bear might be able to shimmy out on the heavy limb, she lowered the pack out of reach.

Sarah returned to the tent and found Dianne asleep. Assured that she had done as much as she could, Sarah crawled into the small space next to Phil and didn't even bother to cover herself.

She didn't know what woke her up in the middle of the night. Ever since she had entered the back country, her hearing had sharpened, especially when she slept.

It took a few moments, but then she realized that it was unusually light outside. The branches of the surrounding trees were silhouetted against the walls of the tent.

She sat up and rubbed the sleep from her eyes, then made her way carefully from the tent so as not to wake Dianne.

The air was far warmer than it had been. When she stood up outside, she saw the moon hanging between the pine trees like a soft white globe. The forest floor was crisscrossed with dark shadows from the trees. A slight breeze was stirring, and it rocked the trees slowly back and forth.

Suddenly, within the moving shadows, she spotted a small animal with a bushy tail. It was tearing through foil packages.

Panicked, Sarah looked up into the trees where she had strung her backpack and saw another raccoon hanging deftly on to the rope with one paw while eating and tossing down food with the other.

Sarah tried to scare the animals away, but they kept eating as if she weren't even there.

She ran to her tent, got her canteen, and threw it at the raccoon on the ground. It slunk back a few feet, but then returned and resumed eating.

In desperation Sarah charged at the animal, but it stood its ground, hissing and snarling viciously as if it would tear her to shreds.

Sarah backed off.

She needed heavier ammunition, so she returned to the tent quickly and took out one of the stretcher poles. Waving the stick in front of her, she made another rush at the animal on the ground, and this time she was able to chase it into the woods.

When she turned around, she heard the raccoon in the tree clawing down the trunk, and then she saw it scamper off.

Fearing the worst, Sarah untied the rope from the tree trunk and lowered the backpack to the ground. When she looked inside, she saw that the raccoons had made a clean sweep of the food, except for some coffee and a few dried prunes. They had obviously been ransacking the pack for some time before she discovered them.

You should have shot the little bastards, Sarah thought as she gathered what little food remained.

She remembered what Rachel had said about the hunger pains and how she should be smart and leave Phil and Dianne behind when things got rough.

You don't have hunger pains yet, Sarah told herself. And you're not going to abandon Phil and Dianne to save your own ass. Hiking to the lodge by yourself is the best thing for everyone.

Sarah stashed the rest of the food inside her jacket. The raccoons would have to fight her for it next time.

As she returned to the tent, she guessed that she could hike to the lodge in two days and could probably make it without any food at all.

But, if it took longer, both she and Dianne would be in greater danger.

Sarah looked at the shotgun leaning against a tree near the tent.

You have to try and hunt some food before you go, she thought. That way, if it takes you a long time to get to the lodge, you and Dianne won't starve to death.

Sarah crawled inside the tent and spread out a pad next to Phil. With the determination to hike to the lodge on her own, and to try to kill some game before she left, Sarah stared at the shadows on the tent until her eyelids grew heavy.

Day Six

With the first light of morning, Sarah woke. She looked at Phil and Dianne and found them still asleep. She left the tent and went outside.

A heavy fog was drifting through the forest, and she could only see the nearest trees. The previous day the forest was frozen and dry, but this morning it was dripping wet. The snow was melting fast. It was sluggish to walk through.

Sarah took her stove and flint from her backpack and boiled some water for coffee. She was glad the raccoons had left the coffee, because it took the morning chill from her bones.

Sarah remembered that morning was one of the best times to spot wildlife, so she quickly finished her coffee, dried off the shotgun with a shirt, and filled the receiver with rifle slugs.

She looked inside the tent, where Phil and Dianne were still both asleep. She thought of leaving a note, but there wasn't anything convenient to write on, so she closed up the tent and started up the slow rise of the hill in front of the campsite.

The snow was dragging on her boots, and she had to lift her legs high to get over it.

As she climbed the hillside, she scanned the trees for any sign of movement. The fog became patchy at times, and she could see fairly well, but then it would close in again, drawing tightly around her.

Suddenly she noticed some tracks in the snow, and she stopped. They were small hoof marks with streaks behind them where the animal had dragged its feet.

Sarah guessed it was a deer.

You don't want anything that big, she thought. A rabbit or a squirrel would be fine, but not a deer.

She followed the trail as she continued to look for smaller game.

By now the wet snow was caked on her legs, and some of it had melted inside her boots. She learned the importance of wearing gaiters in winter hiking.

Pushing through the wet snow was tough work, and Sarah feared it would slow her progress to the lodge. That made it even more important for her to get some food.

She continued to follow the deer trail until it joined up with some others and led her toward the summit of the hill.

Just before she reached the top, she saw something white flash behind some small fir trees. She stopped and looked some more, and eventually could make out not one deer, but two or three.

You have to get closer, she thought. You could shoot into the trees and hope you hit something, but it's not likely. You have to get closer.

With the deer still behind cover, Sarah walked slowly up onto the summit, then took a few cautious steps at a time as she scanned the fir trees for any movement.

They won't stay there forever, she thought. You have to move faster, even if you scare them away.

A thick cloud of fog passed over the hill and blocked Sarah's vision entirely. She took the opportunity to run across the open area that lay between her and the stand of trees until she was fifty or sixty yards away.

As the fog cleared, she threw herself down into the snow and peered over the top.

A moment later, one of the deer broke out into the open as it continued to nibble on the branches.

It was a fawn.

You can't shoot that one, Sarah thought. Even if you were lucky and hit it, you'd never forgive yourself. You'll have to get a lot hungrier before you can shoot something that looks like Bambi.

She watched as two larger deer came out from behind the fir trees and joined the smaller one. The fawn was spotted, but the other two were a grayish brown. All three deer had white bellies and throats, and once in a while they flashed the white patch underneath their stubby tails.

They must be a family, she thought. She pulled the shotgun up alongside her.

124

You're awfully damn close. You might really hit one of them from this close.

I wish the hell I wasn't so close!

The three deer moved slowly and gracefully from branch to branch and tree to tree; then the largest one, which Sarah guessed was the male, moved quickly away.

You can't wait forever, Sarah thought. You've been lucky to get this close. They won't stay around much longer, and you'll never get a better shot than this again.

Just then a dense cloud of fog drifted in front of her eyes and cut off her vision. She half hoped that the deer would move away before the fog cleared again.

You've got to think about running out of food, she thought. You've got to picture yourself hiking all alone through this forest and how much better you'll feel if you have some food with you.

Gradually the fog thinned out, and, when it did, only the female deer remained, with its backside pointed straight at Sarah.

Turn around, she whispered. I'll never hit you with that as a target.

Sarah quietly pumped the forearm of the gun, took off the safety, and aimed at the deer.

As she waited for the animal to move into a better position, Sarah felt afraid. She had never killed anything larger than a bug, and the prospect of real blood and real violence made her wonder about what she was doing.

It's only meat, Sarah tried to convince herself. It's no different from those neat little steaks that you see wrapped up in the supermarket.

Think of it as steaks.

Think of Dianne and Phil . . . and yes, yourself.

Think of those hunger pains.

Finally the doe moved slowly around as it went for another tree. It was almost broadside now.

Squeeze the trigger, Sarah told herself. You'll never get another shot like this.

She wished that the large male deer was the one who had stayed behind.

Trembling, she took a deep breath, then readied herself for the recoil of the gun.

She closed her eyes and fired. When she looked up, the deer was kneeling on its <u>hind</u> legs with blood spreading out

125

onto the white fur of its belly. Suddenly the animal stood up and sprang out of sight into the trees.

Sarah was stunned at first, but then took off after the wounded deer. The deep snow dragged on her legs as she burst through the stand of pine trees and saw the doe leap over the brink of the hill on its way down the other side.

Sarah's heart felt like it was going to burst as she hurdled over the snow, gun in hand, desperately trying to keep up with the deer.

She couldn't see the animal anymore, but the bloody trail was easy to follow.

Fog spread through the forest as Sarah came down the hillside and moved into the hollow, the bright trail of blood leading into a large field of brambles that tripped her and sent her sprawling down. She got up and continued to run until she lost the trail.

Dammit, she said, as her chest heaved and her frosty breath flared from her nostrils. You've lost her. You had the best damn chance in the world, and you lost her!

Sarah looked through the smoky fog until, tired and dejected, she turned around and started slowly back to the campsite.

She had almost cleared the stickers when she heard some rustling off to her right, and, going to investigate, she found the deer tangled up in the brambles, rearing its head and kicking its legs as it tried to get free.

Hurry up and die, Sarah said as she watched from a distance. Die quick and be done with it.

But the animal continued to writhe and kick as the blood leaked from its side. When the deer raised its head and seemed to look straight at Sarah with its large black eyes and its long curling lashes, Sarah knew what she had to do.

She took the safety off the shotgun and walked up next to the animal. Sarah's legs trembled as she raised the barrel of the gun until it was inches from the doe's head.

It would be tougher shooting the animal from so close than it had been to shoot it from a distance.

As soon as the deer settled down into the snow, Sarah fired the gun. The blast took away the top of the skull.

Still shaking and feeling queasy, Sarah was glad the ordeal was over and the poor animal was dead and out of its pain.

Never again, she swore to herself. I'd rather starve.

Sarah pulled the brambles off the carcass, then grabbed the doe's hind legs and dragged the animal out of the thicket and across the snow toward the campsite. It was hard work, and she had to stop and rest several times before she finally pulled the carcass up in front of the tent.

"Is that you, Sarah?" she heard Dianne ask.

Sarah put her gun against a tree and went into the tent on her hands and knees.

Dianne was sitting up inside her sleeping bag. Sarah could plainly see that she was feeling better.

"You had me scared," Dianne said. "I wondered where you were, and then I heard the gun shots."

"I killed a deer," Sarah said.

"Why?"

"Some raccoons got our food last night."

"All of it?"

"Just about, but there's plenty of meat on the deer."

Sarah placed her hand on Phil's head.

"He woke up a minute while you were gone," Dianne said. "He was terribly confused."

"Still, that's good news. And how do you feel?"

"Drained."

"You'll have plenty of time to rest. I'm going to hike to the lodge by myself."

"Are you sure it's the best thing?"

"I'm not sure of anything, but I want to do something."

"Maybe I could carry Phil on the stretcher now that I'm feeling better."

"Forget it. Carrying him yesterday was a waste of time. On my own, I think I can make it to the lodge in two days."

"I hate to think of you all alone."

"I'm the lucky one," Sarah said. "At least I'll be doing something. You have to just sit here and hope I make it."

"Should I give Phil anything if he wakes up again?"

"Water's the most important thing. I'm afraid he's dehydrated."

"I'll get him to drink as much as he can."

"And make sure he stays warm."

"Will do."

"And take care of yourself, too," Sarah said, breaking into a smile.

"You bet."

Sarah paused a moment, then said, "I'm sorry about

Mike. I wanted to tell you earlier, but you weren't in any shape."

"Thanks, Sarah."

"We'll have a long talk about everything as soon as we get back to New York where we belong."

"Sure," Dianne said. "As soon as we get back home."

With that, Sarah left the tent and stood over the carcass.

She remembered the gutted deer she had seen in the back of Lenny's truck at the lodge and how it was slit open through the belly.

It's just like cutting up chicken, Sarah told herself as she removed her hunting knife and knelt down next to the animal.

She jammed the blade through the hide right below the breastbone, then slowly worked it down through the belly.

She was encouraged by how little blood there was, but suddenly the black intestine bulged out through the opening.

Concentrate on what you're doing, Sarah told herself. Don't think about it. Just do it, and that way you won't toss your cookies.

She cut through the black mess, and suddenly it burst loose with a greenish, bloody slime that smelled so acrid and disgusting that Sarah stopped cutting and turned her head away to breathe some fresh air.

You're fucking up bad, Sarah thought. You don't know what the hell you're doing.

She held her breath while she cut down between the legs, as the insides continued to bubble up all over the deer and all over her hands and arms.

She stood up and tried to dump out the deer's insides by yanking on its legs, but not all of the intestine came out, and she had to pull on it with her bare hands.

With the cavity now empty, Sarah turned the deer over on its back and tried to figure out how to get the skin off.

She grabbed hold of the skin near the ribs and pulled it back as she hacked away at the tissue connecting it to the meat.

With much effort, she finally uncovered enough meat to hack off a couple of slabs, but they were covered with the intestinal juices, so she washed them off with water from her canteen.

She lit up her stove and fried the pieces of meat as best

she could; then she put them on an aluminum plate and carried them inside to Dianne.

"Here," she said, handing the plate to Dianne. "Try some."

"Are you sure it's okay?"

"We have to eat something."

"Then you eat first."

Sarah brought a piece of meat to her lips and bit off a little. Her face turned sour instantly.

"What's wrong?" Dianne asked.

"It tastes like shit, that's what wrong."

"Maybe the deer was sick."

"I think I ruined it when I cut open the intestine and got it all over the meat."

"Do you think it can poison us?"

"I don't know, but it's not going to taste very good. I'm going to wait until I get hungrier."

"Me, too."

Sarah told Dianne that she would pack some of the meat in snow inside a backpack and tie it in a tree.

"What if the raccoons come back?" Dianne asked.

"This time I'm going to tie a rope between two trees, then hang the backpack from that. It'll make things tougher for them."

Sarah left the tent and went outside to make her preparations for the hike and to tie up the deer meat and haul the carcass away from the campsite. It was past ten o'clock, and she was disappointed by the late start.

She left the stove and flint for Dianne and took most of the stick matches. She took the shotgun, too, tying it slantwise across the back of her pack.

When she was ready to go, she looked up at the sky and saw a patch of blue through the fog. It was a good sign.

You won't have any trouble heading south if the sun comes out, she thought.

Sarah was worried that she might have walked considerably off course the day before because she had been so tired and the snow had been falling so heavily. But she guessed that, even if she was off by several miles, she was bound to run into the river, and, if she simply followed that, she would eventually find help.

Sarah felt more hopeful about her prospects than she had the day before. When she went to say good-bye to Dianne, both women had tears in their eyes.

Before leaving, Sarah kissed Phil on the cheek. Then she put on her backpack and hiked to the spot where they had stopped walking the previous day. Sarah lined up some trees; then, alone for the first time, she headed confidently into the pine forest.

When the sun broke through a couple of hours later, Sarah took it as another sign of her improving fortune.

Remembering the trick that Mike had taught her, she broke off a twig and pointed the hour hand toward the sun, then found south by running a line between the shadow and twelve o'clock.

She was right on the money!

Sarah took off her parka to avoid sweating; then she continued on her way.

New problems arose to replace the old ones. Although the temperature was warmer, hiking through the slushy snow was hard, and she was getting wet. As she walked, she could hear the water squishing inside her boots.

She was glad she was wearing wool socks.

The most annoying problem was the searing brightness of the sun that reflected off the snow like a mirror and burned into her eyes.

She tried to shade herself by tying a scarf around her forehead so that it hung over her brow, but it wasn't good enough, and her eyes continued to burn.

When she came down into a hollow, she heard the trickling of water, and, searching the area, she discovered a small stream running under the snow. Clearing away the snow to fill her canteen, she noticed some black clay along the bank, and she rubbed some of it under her eyes the way her brother used to do while playing football.

When she stood up and looked across the dazzling white of the snow, she thought the clay did a fair job of cutting the glare. She rubbed on more clay and put some extra in her pack.

Though her legs felt heavy, Sarah forced herself to walk a half hour before taking a break, and she never rested longer than five minutes, except at noon when she took off a full hour to eat.

She stopped on the side of a hill where she could look down at the blanket of pine trees in the hollow. She spread her poncho over a tree stump and sat down.

While she drank water and ate some of the deer meat, Sarah scanned the surrounding countryside.

The hills, the tall pines, the rock, and the blue sky were all quite beautiful, she thought. They were beautiful enough to make her forget momentarily about what a mess she was in.

The air was heavy with pine scent, and she could hear the melting snow.

You're not scared of this anymore, she thought. Here you are sitting in the middle of the wilderness, and you're not scared. You're worried about Phil and worried about finding the lodge and finding it soon, but this place, this wilderness, doesn't worry you at all now, and it used to scare the hell out of you.

I hope I make it to the river today. I know it's asking for a lot, but I'd be damn happy if I could get to the river before dark and know I'm only a day from the lodge.

Just do that for me, God. Do that and make sure that Phil lives, and maybe I won't think you're such a bad guy after all.

Until you dump on me again.

Sarah loaded the shotgun and fired off two rounds.

There was no reply.

She used her watch to make sure she was still heading south; then she put on her backpack and hiked down into the hollow.

As the afternoon wore on, Sarah felt as if the entire forest was melting. The trees were dripping, the rocks were bared, and the melting snow formed a network of streams. One stream seemed to be heading south, so she followed it, encouraged that it grew in size as the miles went by.

Wildlife began to reappear. She saw several birds and an animal that looked like a weasel. She saw deer tracks, but no deer.

She soon became uncomfortably warm because of the bright glare off the snow and had to strip down to her shirt.

As she was hiking she heard a low rumbling sound, and, looking up into the azure sky, she saw the white contrail of a jet airliner.

She knew it was useless to try to signal the plane—she would have had to burn down the entire forest—but she couldn't stop thinking of all the passengers up there drinking and eating while she was hiking for her life.

131

Late in the afternoon, as Sarah was crossing a small meadow in the forest, she came across a pile of deer entrails.

She knew that hunters had been nearby.

She knelt in the snow and felt that the entrails were still frozen on the inside, so she knew that the deer kill wasn't fresh. It had been too warm the previous night for the pile to freeze at all, and she couldn't find the tracks where the carcass had been dragged away.

But it was still good news. Even if the hunters were gone by now, she couldn't be very far from a cabin or a road.

Sarah took off her pack, untied the shotgun, and fired off three rounds in the hope that hunters were close by.

When there was no response, she became worried that her signal would be ignored. Any nearby hunters would think nothing unusual about hearing shotgun fire.

Sarah walked another twenty minutes, and was getting ready to take her usual break, when she heard the stream she was following grow louder just a little way ahead.

She passed up her break and walked farther until the stream tumbled down a series of small waterfalls. When the stream led her to the bank of the river, Sarah shouted jubilantly.

The river was much wider than it had been when the hikers crossed it at a different point several days before. It was big enough to run a boat on. It cut straight through the pine tree forest on the right, but on the left it forked around a small island with a high wooded knob.

Thinking that the water might be shallower at the fork, Sarah hiked upriver until she was standing across from the island.

It was getting close to evening, and Sarah was wondering if it might not be smarter to camp on this side of the river for the night, when she thought she saw something flash at the top of the hill on the island.

Curious, she walked upriver a little more, and as the small clearing at the top of the hill opened, she spotted a cabin with a sheet-metal roof. A thin trail of smoke was rising from the chimney.

Sarah yelled for help, but no one appeared. She loaded three shells into her gun and fired them off.

Still no one.

Why can't someone be home? she thought. You've come so damn close!

132

She thought of staying on the bank and signaling the owner of the cabin when he came back to the island, but she wasn't totally convinced that he wasn't still inside, and, besides, it was getting dark fast, and she might not see him as he came upriver.

Sarah determined to cross right away.

The river was too deep to wade to the island, so she looked around the nearby forest for something to float on. There were some pine trees that had fallen a little way back from the river, and Sarah tried without success to lift one of them.

As she stood wondering what to do, she remembered a painting that hung in her father's study that showed work horses hauling logs out of a forest. It gave Sarah an idea.

She got her rope from the backpack and tied one end to the tree and the other to the metal tubing on her pack frame. Then she put on the harness and began to drag the heavy load through the woods with relative ease, though she had to stop whenever the log snagged on a root or stone. In this way she brought the tree to the edge of the bank, removed the rope, and rolled the tree into the water.

Then she returned and brought down another tree the same way.

It was getting dark and harder to see as Sarah cut two pieces of rope and tied the logs together. The water was ice cold, and Sarah's legs grew numb as she stood with her pants rolled up in the shallows, working on her makeshift raft. When she was finished, she tied the backpack and shotgun to a protruding branch, so that they wouldn't get wet.

As the sun dipped below the treeline, Sarah pointed the raft toward the island, then shoved off hard and jumped aboard.

The heavy raft sank under the water much farther than Sarah had hoped, soaking her pants as she knelt astride the two logs.

The river's current was unexpectedly strong, and Sarah had to paddle briskly in order to get across the fifty yards or so before the current carried her completely past the island.

She was exhausted and chilled by the time the raft grounded a few yards from shore. She untied the backpack and gun from the branch, then waded the rest of the way in.

133

Because of the hill and the trees and rock, the cabin was hidden from view.

The climb looked treacherous, and Sarah had to leave her shotgun and backpack by the river in order to maneuver the slope. The temperature was dropping sharply now that the sun was down, and Sarah shivered as she climbed the hillside by holding on to bushes and rocks and digging her boots into the dirt.

She lost her footing, but managed to hang on to a sapling and pull herself up. She watched the stones she dislodged tumble and crash down the hillside.

Sarah was completely worn out by the time she reached the top of the hill. As soon as she did, she discovered a narrow footpath among the rocks that led all the way from the cabin to a floating dock by the river.

She cursed her stupidity, then jumped down onto the path and followed it to the screened porch in front of the cabin.

The door to the porch was open, and she went inside, where there was a stack of split logs, some busted patio furniture, and a tool box.

A large picture window looked out over the river. Sarah peered inside to make sure no one was home; then she tried to open the door.

It was locked.

Sarah was getting terribly cold, so she went to the tool box, found a screwdriver and a hammer, and opened the front door by driving the screwdriver between the lock and the jam.

She went inside and felt the warmth coming from the wood stove in the back of the room. There was a large living area behind the picture window on the right side, with a kitchen and dining area to the left. The cabin was furnished with torn upholstered chairs and some end tables made from local timber. The walls were pine-paneled, the floors oak. There were paintings of wildlife on the walls, and against the back wall there was a large map.

Sarah had the feeling that a woman had decorated the cabin for a man, but for some reason the place had been allowed to run down.

Sarah turned on the petcock to the lamp above the dining table, but the light didn't go on. She could hear gas escaping from the lamp, so she lit one of her matches and held it to the mantles. They flamed up, then settled down into a bright glow.

In the harsh light she saw dirty dishes all over the kitchen. There was a small propane refrigerator next to the sink, and a three-burner range next to the window.

Sarah went to the back of the room and opened the door to the wood stove. There were only a couple of burned logs in the bottom, so she went out on the porch to get some more.

She piled several logs on the fire, but nothing happened. So she closed the iron door, and opened the damper on the stove pipe, and a few minutes later she heard the wood catch fire, and the stove began to roar.

When the heat began to radiate throughout the room, she closed the damper and the draft at the bottom of the stove. She warmed herself for a few minutes, then went off to explore the cabin and see if she could find some dry clothes.

She entered the first room on the left and lit the propane lamp against the wall. She found a bed and dresser and, on the opposite wall, some shelves filled with hunting and men's magazines.

There was a broken window in the room that was covered with plastic to keep out the cold.

Sarah moved on to the second room in the rear of the cabin where she found a yellowed sink and toilet and, much to her delight, a shower stall.

She immediately turned on the water. It came out ice cold at first, but then it turned into a steamy spray.

Ecstatic at the prospect of a hot shower, Sarah quickly shed her clothes on the floor and stepped into the stall.

The first contact of her tight skin with the hot water felt glorious, and Sarah turned around slowly under the spray, letting the water warmly massage the stiff muscles in the back of her neck.

She closed her eyes and dreamed that she was in her apartment in New York.

It was several minutes later that Sarah finally picked up a bar of soap and began to wash off a week's accumulation of dirt and sweat.

She reached her hand between her legs and took out her tampon. It was dark with old blood. She opened the shower curtain and dropped the tampon in the toilet bowl.

135

Sarah continued to shower until she felt the water begin to cool. Then she quickly rinsed herself, turned off the faucets, and started to leave.

When she pulled back the shower curtain, Sarah shrieked and covered herself up.

Standing in the bathroom doorway, wearing dayglow orange hunters' caps and holding rifles in their hands, their eyes raw, hungrily taking in what they saw, were Bill and Lenny, the two men from the lodge.

"I'll be darned," Lenny said grinning. "It's one of those New York people."

"I believe you're right," Bill said.

"What are you doing here?" Lenny asked threateningly. "Where's that big fella?"

Sarah started to answer, but the two rifles made her change her mind.

"Mike and the others are exploring the island," she lied.

Lenny stared at her suspiciously.

"Would you mind getting out while I get dressed?" Sarah asked.

Lenny glanced down into the toilet bowl, then turned to Sarah and said, "We'll be waiting for you in the other room."

He spat a wad of tobacco juice into the toilet bowl; then he motioned for Bill to leave.

As soon as the two men were gone and the door was closed, Sarah quickly got out of the shower stall and put on her clothes. Her wool pants were wet and cold.

Sarah was frightened by the two men and wanted to get away from the cabin and the island as soon as she could, but she had to worry about getting help for Dianne and Phil.

It had been smart not to tell them about Mike and Jim, she thought. Even though the hunters were suspicious, she had planted the seed of doubt in their minds, and it might give her the protection she needed.

Before going back into the main room, Sarah constructed a plan of action and made sure that her knife was out of sight underneath the parka.

When she thought she looked composed, she opened the door.

Lenny was sitting in one of the upholstered chairs with his rifle in his lap, while Bill was cutting up what looked like deer meat on the kitchen table.

"I'm going to see what's taking the others so long," Sarah said as she walked straight for the wall map and began to take it down.

Lenny stood up.

"Mike promised to show me how to read a contour map," Sarah continued. "He can teach me how to get around the island with this."

She rolled the map up and started to leave, but Lenny blocked her path.

"This island's no bigger than a dot on that map," Lenny said. "And it's pitch dark outside."

The room was hot from the wood stove, and Sarah could smell Lenny's rancid clothes.

"He might want to look at it anyway," Sarah said. She could tell that her voice was shaking.

"Sit down," Lenny said.

Sarah was startled.

"If your friends are really out there," Lenny said, "then they'll be back shortly."

"They have flashlights," Sarah said.

Lenny nudged her over in the direction of the chairs.

"Sit down," he said again.

Reluctantly Sarah took the map over to the chair closest to the door.

"Mike said that he wouldn't be gone very long," Sarah said.

"You better hope he's not gone very long," Lenny said.

He spat across the room at the stove, then walked to the kitchen table. Bill was pounding three large steaks with the side of an iron skillet.

"What do you suppose really happened to her people?" Bill said.

Lenny looked back over at Sarah and spoke loud enough for her to hear. "I think they got themselves killed. That's what I think."

When the frying pan on the stove began to smoke, Bill threw on the steaks. They spattered and sent up a cloud of steam. Bill's eyes glowed as he tended the iron skillet.

Sarah wondered how many steps it would take to get through the door.

You have to move soon, she thought. If you can get down the footpath, and if they left the boat at the dock, you might get away.

Lenny was still holding his weapon. Bill's rifle was leaning near the refrigerator . . . far out of reach.

Sarah's heart quickened as she imagined herself hurtling down the hillside while dodging the hunters' gunfire. Her chances were damn poor.

Suddenly Lenny walked over to her and placed the end of his rifle against Sarah's forehead.

Her mouth went dry.

"Your friends are dead, aren't they?" Lenny said.

"I told you that they're exploring the island."

"They're not exploring anything."

Lenny lowered the barrel of the rifle onto Sarah's chest.

"I saw your tits when you were in the shower," he said. "They're kind of small, but you have nice big nipples."

Lenny pointed the barrel at Sarah's breast.

"Take off that jacket," he ordered.

"No, I won't."

"How would you like me to shoot your tits off?"

Bill started laughing on the other side of the room.

"That's real funny," he said. "That's a good one!"

Sarah thought of reaching for her knife, but she knew it would be a futile move.

"You heard me," Lenny said. "Take it off!"

Sarah started slowly unzipping the parka. Her hands were shaking so badly that she had trouble opening it.

She had no doubt that Lenny was capable of killing her—his eyes were as cold and hard as the glass eyes in a game trophy.

When she was finished with the jacket, Lenny told her to open her shirt. She unbuttoned the top three buttons; then Lenny pushed back her shirt with the end of the gun, exposing Sarah's breasts.

"Now take it off all the way," he said, "and take your pants off while you're at it."

Sarah slowly unbuttoned her shirt and started to unbuckle her pants when the door suddenly opened and a huge man wearing a dark hooded parka walked inside.

He held a rifle under one arm.

When he threw back the hood, Sarah saw that it was the owner of the lodge—Bob Harwood.

"Get away from her," he ordered Lenny.

"What the hell's eating you?"

"I said get away!"

Harwood looked at Sarah and said, "What are you doing here? Where's Mike?"

"He's dead. He and Jim were killed in a climbing accident. Phil's hurt badly and needs help."

"What about the others?"

"Dianne's staying with Phil where I left them. Rachel's lost."

Harwood nodded his head slowly, then looked at Lenny and said, "Get out of here."

"What the hell are you talking about?"

"I said to get out!"

Bill was sitting at the table eating his supper. He told Harwood to cool down and come and join him.

"I want you out, too," Harwood said.

Sarah was tremendously relieved. She buttoned her shirt and walked away from Lenny.

"We're not leaving this cabin at night," Lenny said.

"That's what you think."

Harwood raised his rifle so it was pointed right at Lenny's chest.

"We can have it out now if you want to," he said.

Lenny's face reddened.

"I don't want to fight you," he said. "Why are you getting all steamed up just because I want some pussy? We can both have a piece of her, then dump her ass in the woods. Everyone will think she got lost and died."

"I'm not going to tell you again," Harwood said.

"Come on," Bill said, getting up from the table. "Let's go."

"You owe us a lot," Lenny told Harwood. "Don't you forget that."

"I don't owe you shit. That favor's been paid."

Bill already had his coat and orange cap on. He grabbed his rifle and headed for the door.

"Come on," he told Lenny. "Let's get going. We can take the boat to Chrisman's old place and stay there for the night."

Lenny looked at Harwood's rifle again, then snorted and went for his gear.

Harwood kept his rifle slung loosely across his arm as he watched the men throw together their things.

"And take that buck you got this morning," Harwood said. "It's rightfully yours."

Lenny threw his rucksack over his shoulder and picked up his weapon.

"This is one hell of a way to treat your friends," Lenny said.

He glared at Sarah threateningly; then he grabbed a bottle of gin off the table and went for the door.

"You haven't seen the last of us," Lenny said. "There's a lot of river between here and the lodge."

He spat on the floor, then left the cabin right behind Bill. As soon as Sarah heard the screen door close, she turned to Harwood and said, "Thank God you showed up when you did. What are you doing here?"

"Me and Lenny and Bill was hunting together," Harwood said. "This evening I stayed behind hoping a buck we saw earlier would show up again, but it didn't."

Harwood put down his rifle, took off his jacket, and reached up on the shelf above the refrigerator for a bottle of whiskey. He grabbed a tin mug and sat down at the table.

"Eat that other steak," Harwood said.

"I'm too nervous to eat."

She heard the faint sound of a motorboat down by the dock.

"Do you have more than one boat?" she asked.

"Yeah, there's another one."

"I'd like to leave right away if we can," Sarah said.

"Bring that map over here," Harwood said as he started eating the steak that Bill had cooked for him.

Sarah picked up the map from the chair where she had left it and spread it out next to Harwood's plate.

"Do you remember passing a high cliff?" Harwood asked.

"Yeah, that's where Mike and Jim were killed."

Harwood stuck his knife at the spot on the map.

"See where the contour lines run together close?" he said.

"Yes."

"That's the face of the cliff. Where the lines start spreading apart down through here is the hollow leading to the bald hill."

"And the hill is where the circles are."

"You got it. And this spot here, just south, is the meadows."

140

"I bet I left Dianne and Phil about here," Sarah said pointing at some recognizable terrain. "I'm sure we didn't get far carrying the stretcher."

"We'll go to the lodge in the morning," Harwood said. "I'll call up the Trout Run station, and they can get a helicopter out to your friends in a few hours."

"Can't we go tonight?"

"Too dark. We have to travel several hours on the river, and there are some narrows that are too dangerous to run at night."

He stuck a big piece of meat in his face and kept talking as he chewed.

"Do your friends have any food?"

"Yes."

"And a tent?"

"Yes."

"Then don't worry about them. They'll be fine till tomorrow."

"I can't help worrying. I think Phil has a skull fracture."

"There's nothing you can do about it right now, so sit tight."

Sarah didn't like the delay a bit, but she didn't see any other way.

"Eat some of this venison," Harwood told her, pointing to the steak that was meant for Lenny.

"I think I'd rather have some coffee."

"Help yourself."

While Harwood finished his steak, Sarah boiled some water on the stove and made some instant coffee.

Harwood was eating hungrily. The juice from the meat was running down his chin and hands, and once in a while he'd wipe his hands across his chest.

Sarah brought her cup of coffee over in front of the picture window and looked outside. She could see the crescent moon rising above the treeline, and she could see the moonlight reflecting off the river between the dark contours of the hills.

"You have quite a view here," she said.

"Me and a few other fellas got together and built six cabins along the river about ten years ago. My wife and I used to come up here a lot."

"Mike told me about your wife dying. I'm sorry."

Harwood didn't say anything. He got up from the table

and went over to one of the greasy upholstered chairs in the living area. He put his cup of whiskey down on the table next to him and reached for his pipe and tobacco pouch.

"I guess you're married to that fella in the woods," he said as he stuffed the bowl.

"He's a good friend."

"I see."

Harwood struck a match on his boot heel and lit up his pipe. "I'm damn sorry about Mike," he said. "We had a good time hunting last year."

"Mike told me about it."

"I bet he didn't tell you everything," Harwood said, breaking into a grin.

"I wouldn't know."

"Mike was quite a ladies' man. He spent half the hunting trip shacked up with some gal in town."

"I'm not surprised."

"He brought his girlfriend back to the cabin where we were staying and had her take all her clothes off in front of us. Some of the boys even took her into the bedroom."

Harwood looked up at Sarah as if to study her reaction.

"I guess that sort of thing's as common as a housefly in New York," he said.

"Not the New York where I live," Sarah said.

"I heard about those disco places where everyone takes his clothes off."

"Don't believe everything you hear. New York's probably no different from Montreal or Toronto."

"There's a lot of goings-ons there, too, believe me."

Sarah emptied her cup and put it down on the windowsill.

She was tired of the conversation, as well as physically tired.

"I think I'd like to go to bed now," she told Harwood.

Harwood got up from his chair and went to the closet between the two rooms in the back. He took down a blanket and handed it to Sarah.

"You can use my bed," he said.

"That's all right. I'll sleep in the chair."

"No, go ahead. I'm gonna stay up awhile and do some sipping."

"Okay. Thanks."

She started to go into the bedroom, then turned toward

Harwood and said, "You don't think that Lenny and Bill will give us trouble tomorrow, do you?"

"No," Harwood said. "They won't give us any trouble."

Sarah wished him a goodnight.

"When you take your clothes off," Harwood said, "hand them to me, and I'll put them next to the stove, so they'll dry overnight."

"Thanks. I'll do that."

Sarah entered the room, threw the blanket on the bed, and took off her wet things. Wearing her plaid flannel shirt and bikini briefs, she stood behind the door and opened it just wide enough to pass the clothes through.

Then she wished Harwood goodnight again and went to turn off the propane lamp on the wall. She closed the petcock, and, as the glow in the mantles died, she hopped into bed and pulled the layers of blankets up to her chin.

In the other room, she could hear Harwood going through the refrigerator. There was a gap at the top of the door about five inches wide, that Sarah guessed was there to let in the heat from the other room. A shaft of light shot through the gap and struck the wall right above Sarah's head.

She thought about Dianne and Phil still out in the forest and felt sorry that they didn't know she had found help. They were so close to being rescued now. But Sarah didn't want to think about that—it was too exciting, and she'd never get to sleep.

To push everything else out of her mind, Sarah thought about her cat, Christabel. She pictured herself sitting on the sofa in her apartment, stroking Christabel's soft white fur and listening to the soothing hum of her motor.

The warm memory soon lulled Sarah to sleep.

Day Seven

Sarah woke the following morning when the light coming through the broken window crossed her eyes. She thought it was awfully bright outside, and looking at her watch she was shocked to see that it was past nine.

She threw off the covers and went to the door. When she opened it slightly, she saw that Harwood was in the bathroom, so she took the opportunity to dash out and get her clothes.

When she put on her pants, she noticed that her knife and sheath were missing from the belt.

She became worried when, after returning to the living room, she heard Harwood throwing up and coughing. Finally he opened the bathroom door and came stumbling out dressed in his baggy longjohns.

He looked up at her with his bloodshot eyes and wiped some vomit off his chin.

"I thought we were leaving early," Sarah said.

From the way that Harwood was staring at her, she knew she was in trouble.

"There's no rush," Harwood said as he came toward her. "Let's you and me bed down together for a while."

Instantly Sarah ran for the door, but it was locked. She shook it violently; then Harwood grabbed her from behind and threw her down on the hard floor.

She screamed and kicked, but Harwood suddenly punched her in the face. She heard the crisp snap of her nose and felt the hot pain rush into the back of her head.

Harwood put his knee on her stomach and bore down with all his weight. While the blood gushed from her nose, Sarah fought for air and flailed her arms and kicked her legs, straining against the weight, trying to dig her nails into Harwood's flesh as he managed to pull down her pants below the knee, then yanked her right leg out and clutched her throat with one hand while spreading her thighs with the other, and finally wedged himself between her legs, still strangling Sarah so hard that she gagged and foamed, her eyes exploding from the pressure in her skull, and she squeezed her thighs together and threw herself from side to side, but Harwood tightened his grip on her throat, and dropped his longjohns, and fell down on top of Sarah, groping and spreading, driving himself into her so hard that he slammed her head into the table leg, and she reached up desperately and grabbed hold of the table while Harwood thrust madly, his face red, grunting and puffing, and Sarah pulled the table over, crashing it to the floor, just as Harwood rammed into her, cracking her joints, seeming to split her open in a final frenzied assault.

Suddenly he lay quiet.

Sarah felt the grasp on her throat loosen, and she gulped for air. As she shoved off Harwood's suffocating weight, she felt him withdraw. She squirmed out from underneath and sat with her back against the fallen table, trying to catch her breath and bring the room into focus.

Harwood slowly picked himself up on his feet and pulled up his longjohns from his knees.

Sarah cried as she put on her trousers.

"Get in the bedroom," Harwood ordered.

Sarah hesitated, and Harwood grabbed her by the hair and shoved her toward the door. He threw her inside the room and slammed the door. She could hear a key turn in the lock.

Her nose continued to bleed freely. Sarah ripped off a piece of the bedsheet and held it to her nostrils, lifting back her head to stop the flow.

She went to the mirror on top of the dresser and took a look at herself. Her nose was crooked and loose-jointed, like a broken chicken wing.

She began to cry again and sat down on the edge of the bed as she continued to try to stop the bleeding.

For several minutes she sat dazed and terrified by what had happened, but, when she heard Harwood moving around in the other room, she knew she had to act quickly.

Don't fall apart, she told herself. Hang on to yourself hard and keep it all right in front of you in one piece. Block out everything but what you are right now—not one minute ago or five—but right now, totally now.

Slowly her fear turned to anger. The anger focused her emotions and took away the other feeling that made her weak and helpless.

Her nose finally stopped bleeding, and Sarah went to the bedroom window and tore away the plastic covering. She tried to unlock the window, but it was rusted shut.

The only way to get out was to break the rest of the glass, but Harwood might come in at any moment.

Sarah brought a chair over to the bedroom door and stood up to look outside through the gap.

She could see Harwood getting dressed on the other side of the room. She continued to watch as he got his rifle out from the closet and took it over in front of the picture window, where he sat down and stared outside.

Sarah stepped down off the chair and went to the bed. She took off the pillow case and wrapped it around her hand. Then she went to the window and gingerly broke off the first shard of glass. She listened carefully to see if Harwood responded to the noise, but then, confident that he hadn't heard anything, she set the glass on the bed and broke off another large piece.

She was working on one of the last pieces of glass when it fell to the ground and shattered.

Sarah froze and listened for Harwood in the other room. She was sure he had heard the noise, but, when she climbed onto the chair to take a look, he was still sitting in front of the picture window staring outside.

Sarah breathed with relief and went back to work on the window.

When the last piece was removed, Sarah crawled out of the window and jumped to the ground.

She knew that Harwood would see her if she tried to make it to the boat. From the picture window there was a clear view of the footpath and the dock.

Sarah climbed the rise behind the cabin and worked her way through the pine trees and over the rocky ground until she arrived at the top of the slope where she had left her hiking gear.

She wanted to move fast, but the slope was dangerous, and she had to thread her way down the rock carefully, taking her time to set her feet firmly, and being cautious about which saplings she held on to.

Finally she made it and discovered her backpack and shotgun where she had left them.

The temperature was warm for a fall day; the sun was bright. Sarah was glad for the weather because she knew there was only one way to escape fast enough—she had to swim.

The water was biting cold. Sarah knew that she would only have five or ten minutes to make the forty-yard swim before she froze.

She wanted to take her backpack across, so she would have food and dry clothing. And she wanted to take the shotgun, too, in case Harwood came after her, or if she ran into Bill and Lenny downriver. But the swim would be hard enough without the extra weight.

Hoping for last minute luck, Sarah looked around the woods for something to float on but came up empty.

As she stood by the water's edge and looked into the river, she recalled the still vivid experience of having almost drowned at the pond. It made what she had to do far more difficult.

Take a breath and go! she told herself. Don't think about anything. Just get in there and swim!

Sarah removed her boots and stepped out into the shallow water. She tried to ease herself slowly into the river, but, when that failed, she took a deep breath and dove straight in, and started swimming furiously for the other bank.

The cold hit her like a kick in the ribs. Her wool pants quickly became soaked and heavy.

When Sarah looked up to measure her progress, she heard a loud humming sound to her left, and turning she was stunned to see Bob Harwood in his motorboat cruising straight for her, throwing a large wake to either side.

Sarah swam madly for the bank, but, before she could get there, Harwood raced his boat right in front of her, splashing the wake into her face, making her choke on the water. She coughed raspingly as she treaded on the surface, and her body grew heavier and less responsive. Harwood circled the boat wildly, drowning Sarah in the wake, cutting off her attempts to break through to the other side.

Soon everything turned into a terrifying whirl of frothy water and the shrill whine of the motorboat and the mad look in Harwood's eyes as he continued to circle, and Sarah finally let go and slipped under the water.

Looking up at the choppy surface of the river and the

careening hull of the boat, Sarah stretched her arms for the light as her ears began to hum louder and louder, and at last she fell unconscious.

She had no idea how much later it was when she came to inside the bedroom of the cabin. Harwood had stripped her of everything, including her watch, and she lay naked under the covers. The window was boarded up with plywood.

Her rear end was burning and sore, and she was certain that Harwood had raped her again while she was unconscious.

Sarah wished that she had drowned in the river. The thought of Harwood coming through that door to beat and rape her again was the most horrifying thought imaginable.

How long would he torture her until he finally killed her? He was bound to kill her in the end, and he could do it with impunity because there were a thousand places he could bury her in the back country, and her body would never be found.

Sarah's fear turned into rage. She wanted to make Harwood suffer as much as she had suffered. She wanted to kill him.

Sarah threw off the covers and wrapped herself in a blanket. Then she brought a chair over to the door and stood up on it to look outside.

Harwood was sleeping near the wood stove, his rifle set across his lap.

Sarah stepped down from the chair and quietly tried to open the door.

It was locked.

Still wrapped in the blanket, she got down and began to go through the dresser drawers. She found Harwood's soiled clothes, some fishing lures, and other junk, but then she discovered some women's clothing in the bottom drawer.

She quickly put on a shirt, a pair of jeans, and some wool socks. In the back of the drawer there was an envelope filled with newspaper clippings. She carried them over to the door, so she could see in the light.

All of the stories concerned the accidental hunting death of Clara Harwood and the subsequent inquest.

Then Sarah saw a photograph of Bill and Lenny at the

149

top of one of the stories. They looked strangely out of place in dark suits. Reading the story, Sarah learned that Bill and Lenny had testified that Clara Harwood had stepped into her husband's line of fire the day of the accident.

Sarah was more convinced than ever that she would be killed. She went to put the clippings on the bed, and when she did she stepped on something soggy. Reaching down in the dark, she discovered her wet clothes.

She kicked them aside and stood up on the chair.

Harwood was still asleep.

Sarah was determined to stop him the next time he came in to rape her, so she looked around the dark room for something to use as a weapon.

She thought of hitting him with the chair as he came through the door, but she doubted that it would stop him for long.

She thought of breaking the mirror and stabbing him with one of the shards, but the mirror was too brittle and would never pierce deeply enough.

The only way that Sarah could think of to stop a man of Harwood's strength and size was to get her hands on his rifle.

She pictured herself jumping on him as he came through the door or tripping him up somehow, but each time she imagined a different sequence, the result was the same—Harwood overpowering her and raping and beating her again.

She thought of rushing by him and racing for the front door, but she was certain that the door was locked, and she would never be able to jump out a window before Harwood caught up with her.

She became convinced that there was no way for her to save her life.

Sarah went back and sat on the bed. She started to cry again. Every part of her body was aching and sore.

The darkness of the room made Sarah even more fearful. She wished she had some matches, so she could turn on the lamp.

She went to the wall and opened the petcock on the lamp. For a while, she listened to the slow escape of the gas; then she brightened up as she thought of a plan.

She guessed that propane was different from natural gas in some ways, but she hoped it might be the same in one way—explosive power.

She searched the room desperately for matches—under the bed, inside the drawers, on the windowsill. Then she remembered the matches in her pants pockets and went to get her wet clothes.

Sure enough the matches were still there! And they were dry inside the waterproof canister.

Sarah went back to the lamp and opened the petcock as far as it would go, letting the gas run freely. She struck a match to her zipper, and, when she held it to the lamp, there was a loud WHOMP and a bright blue flame.

Sarah's excitement soon vanished as she considered some of the problems of her plan. One of them was the gap at the top of the door. The gas would never explode unless the room was sealed.

Sarah took one of the blankets off the bed, brought the chair against the door, and stood up to look outside. Through the gap, she could see Harwood stirring as if he might wake up, but then he settled down again.

Sarah crammed the blanket into the opening, then went to the lamp to make certain that the cock was opened full. That accomplished, she went and sat down on the edge of the bed and listened to the slow hissing sound.

There was nothing left to do but wait.

It seemed to take forever, but Sarah finally caught the first strong scent of gas. Her elation soon ended though, when she considered the possibility that the propane might be toxic.

She wasn't sure whether it was her imagination, but ten minutes or so later she felt dizzy and sick to her stomach.

When she tried to stand up from the bed, she fell on the floor. She was disoriented—the walls of the room were spinning.

Afraid that she would soon pass out, Sarah crawled to the chair by the door and stood up. She desperately pulled back the blanket and breathed the fresh air rushing into the room.

When her mind and vision had cleared enough, she brought Harwood into focus. He was moving around restlessly in his sleep. The rifle dropped off his lap, and the noise made him wake with a start.

As he rubbed his eyes, Sarah stuffed the blanket back into the gap, jumped down from the chair, and stood behind the door.

A moment later, she heard Harwood fumbling with the key.

Sarah didn't make a sound. She wanted Harwood to think she was still in bed.

Suddenly the door opened, and Harwood walked deep into the room. He turned, facing her. His eyes grew wide. He swung his rifle up from the hip.

Sarah pivoted into the doorway, and struck the match to her zipper, and the bedroom exploded in a bright blue ball of fire, slamming the door into Sarah's face, throwing her to the floor.

It took her a moment to realize that her arm was on fire, and she turned over on her side, rocking back and forth until the flames went out.

The explosion had blown the blanket out from the gap at the top of the door, and black smoke was pouring into the room as Sarah got up and ran to the kitchen window.

Just as she picked up one of the chairs to smash out the window, the bedroom door crashed open, and Harwood stood facing her like a huge, smoldering bear, the skin on his face charred and peeled, his hair smoking.

He tried to speak, but only a black, gurgling foam escaped his lips.

As Harwood lumbered toward her, rifle still in hand, Sarah smashed out the window with the chair and dove outside onto the ground. The fall stunned her momentarily; then she sprang up and ran at breakneck speed down the winding footpath all the way to the dock, where she fought with the moorings as Harwood came staggering down the hillside, his clothes still smoking, and Sarah threw off the ropes, jumped into the aluminum boat, and tried to start the motor, yanking on the cord until she realized that there wasn't a gas can in the boat.

She looked up the hillside just as Harwood fired his rifle. The shot went wild, clipping off a branch from a nearby tree.

Terrified, Sarah shoved off from the dock and scrambled into the bow, where she began to paddle furiously, trying to move the boat away from the island, but Harwood staggered onto the dock, aimed, and fired. The shot slapped right next to the boat, and a second shot ripped through the transom.

Sarah crouched low in the boat and watched Harwood

aim the rifle again. Suddenly his knees gave out, and he buckled to the deck, then tumbled into the river like a big log.

Sarah watched the water until Harwood's body failed to surface; then she hurriedly paddled the rest of the way to shore.

As soon as she was on the bank, she tore the sleeve off her shirt to check her burned arm. The skin was covered with small blisters, but it didn't really hurt yet. She splashed some cold water on her arm, then started running along the river, mindless of her stocking feet.

It was early afternoon now. The temperature was warm, and the ground was spongy from the melted snow.

Sarah ran until she fell down exhausted and buried her face in the pine needles.

She lay there a minute catching her breath, waiting for the cramp to go away in her side. Then she got up and went to the river to quench her thirst.

Her thinking had cleared enough now to realize that she could go back to the cabin and be certain of finding food and staying warm for the night. But the very idea of going back was repulsive beyond all measure. It didn't matter that Harwood was dead.

Sarah started walking again. She walked one hour, two hours, until, stopping to drink, she heard the nearby sound of gunfire.

She jumped up the side of the bank and started running toward the area where the shots had come from. She felt giddy and light-headed.

She ran through a stand of small pines and broke out on the bank of a cove along the river. When she saw two men in a boat on the other side, with their backs turned toward her, Sarah yelled to catch their attention. But when she saw their dayglow orange hunters' caps, she froze.

She was going to turn and run when one of the men in the boat looked at her. It wasn't Lenny, and it wasn't Bill. It was an older man with a white beard and sunglasses.

Sarah waved to him as tears rolled from her eyes. She dropped to her knees.

By the time the men crossed the cove in the boat and jumped out onto the bank, Sarah was laughing and crying all at the same time.

The bearded man told her to lie down, and he checked her for injuries and asked her medical questions as the other man talked to someone on a portable radio.

"You're going to be fine now," the bearded man told her. "You're in good shape."

The other rescuer spent the next ten minutes cutting down trees with a chainsaw until Sarah heard the approaching sound of a helicopter, and, looking up into the trees, she soon spotted it hovering overhead.

The men lit up a flare, and red smoke drifted across the landing area.

Sarah tried to stand up.

"Stay put," she was told. "You deserve to be chauffeured for a while after what you've been through."

The helicopter landed, stirring up a whirlwind of leaves and pine needles, and two men in yellow helmets and jumpsuits scrambled out of the door and came running toward Sarah with a stretcher.

They shouted to each other above the deafening whine of the motor, then rolled Sarah onto the stretcher, covered her with some blankets, and hustled her into the clearing and up into the helicopter.

As the noise of the engine grew louder, the bearded man waved to Sarah and jumped outside. The door was slammed shut, and immediately after, Sarah felt the helicopter lift clumsily off the ground, then tilt steeply forward as it climbed into the sky.

In all the noise and confusion, Sarah had completely forgotten about the other hikers.

She grabbed the arm of one of the men and shouted, "Some of my friends are still out there!"

"They're all right," he shouted back and gave the thumbs-up sign. Then he went over to speak to the other crewman.

Twenty minutes later, the helicopter landed in a field near a rural hospital, and Sarah was rushed into the emergency room, where she was met by a team of doctors and nurses. They cut off her clothes, treated her for rape, and set her nose.

She was cleaned up, given a gown and a bracelet, then taken to one of the wards.

When she asked the nurse about her friends, the nurse told her not to worry.

"All you need to think about is rest for the next few days," she said.

And to reinforce the message, she gave Sarah a sedative that knocked her out within minutes.

The Aftermath

Sarah spent the next two days in a fog, not caring about herself or anyone else.

She drifted in and out of sleep, dreaming about Phil, and Gary, and her father, dreaming about the horrors of the last week.

On the morning of her third day in the hospital, Sarah was rested and alert enough to ask questions.

She learned that Phil and Dianne had been rescued the day she had left them to hike to the river. A local trapper had found the red shirt she had tied in the trees, giving directions, and he had gotten in touch with the RCMP. Phil and Dianne were picked up just before dark.

Sarah learned more about her own rescue, too—how the search had started in earnest the following dawn and progressed most of the day without results. Finally, a rescue party spotted the burning cabin, and they found tracks along the bank.

All that remained was to search downriver. The rest Sarah knew.

There was still no word about Rachel Wheatley.

Sarah was questioned by the police for over an hour. They were especially interested in what she had to tell them about Bill and Lenny and their involvement in the possible murder of Clara Harwood.

"I hope this ugly business doesn't keep you from visiting Canada again," one of the investigators said.

"Right," Sarah said. "Sure thing."

In the afternoon, Sarah was given a robe and placed in a wheelchair, then taken down the hall to visit with Phil for the first time.

She felt nervous going down the hall, but, when she went into the room and saw Phil over by the window, she jumped out of the wheelchair and hugged him.

155

For a minute, they were too overwhelmed to speak.

"You sure look good," Phil said.

"You look all right yourself."

One of Phil's legs was in traction, and he had a bandage on his head from surgery.

"So how are you?" Phil asked excitedly.

"I'm just glad it's all over with."

Phil tapped the cast on his leg.

"I suppose you heard about my leg," he said. "A brace won't be too bad. I'm lucky to be alive."

"I'm sure that Mike and Jim would agree."

"I still can't believe that they're dead."

"Neither can I."

Phil took Sarah's hand.

"You saved my life," he told her.

"In a way, we're even now. You saved my life once."

"When was that?"

"After Gary left me."

"As soon as you and I get back to New York, I think we should have a long talk," Phil said.

"We've had long talks before."

"But this time it'll be an honest talk."

"Okay," Sarah said. "We'll have a long, honest talk."

Phil and Sarah smiled at each other. It was the kind of smile that passes between friends.

Epilogue

Rachel's body was found two days later. She had died of exposure.

One week after Sarah returned to New York, a boy in the neighborhood showed up on her doorstep with a ruffled and scratched but otherwise healthy cat named Christabel.

Dianne Stove remarried three months after the loss of her husband.

Over the next year, Sarah and Phil saw each other with growing infrequency, until Sarah applied for and received a promotion to the Portland office, and her relationship with Phil came to an end.